OLEG KASHIN

FARDWOR, RUSSIA!

A Fantastical Tale of Life Under Putin

Translated from the Russian by Will Evans

Introduction by Max Seddon

RESTLESS BOOKS
BROOKLYN, NEW YORK

Copyright © 2010 Oleg Kashin
Translation copyright © 2012 Will Evans
Introduction copyright © 2015 Max Seddon

First published in Russian as *Roissya Vperde: Fantasticheskaya Povest*
by Ad Marginem, Moscow, 2010
Digital edition published by Restless Books, 2016
This edition published by Restless Books, 2016

Cover design by Rodrigo Corral
Set in Garibaldi by Tetragon, London

Library of Congress Cataloging-in-Publication
Data: Available upon request.

ISBN: 978-1-63206-039-6

Printed in the United States of America

Ellison, Stavans, and Hochstein LP
232 3rd Street, Suite A111
Brooklyn, NY 11215
www.restlessbooks.com
publisher@restlessbooks.com

This is a work of fiction. Names, characters, businesses,
places, events and incidents are either the products of the
author's imagination or used in a fictitious manner.

FARDWOR,
RUSSIA!

OLEG KASHIN AND
FARDWOR, RUSSIA!

An Introduction by Max Seddon,
World Correspondent for BuzzFeed News

YOU CAN JUST ABOUT see the metal rod the first man is holding, hidden in a bouquet of flowers, on the surveillance tape as he follows Oleg Kashin near the writer's home in Moscow. As Kashin approaches a gate, a second man appears, and the two proceed to beat him violently for a solid sixty seconds. The flowers fly off, exposing the metal rod. There's no sound in the grainy black-and-white footage of Kashin's attack, just an image of him writhing on the ground, trying to roll away from his pursuers and shield himself with his hands, then crawling unsteadily forward after the men leave him, alone in the dark, and tumbling onto the pavement.

The attempt on Kashin's life on November 6, 2010, was unmistakably provoked by his work at *Kommersant*, then

Russia's top daily newspaper; symbolically, the two men worked over his hands, as if to ensure he couldn't write any more.[1] Kashin lost the tip of his left pinky finger in the attack and spent several days in a coma with a concussion, multiple fractures, and a broken jaw. It was only the latest of dozens of attacks on journalists in Russia over the past few decades, an act that has become all too commonplace—as has the inevitable cover-up. Intrepid reporters anger government officials by exposing wrongdoing, and those same officials then order the assaults and manipulate the justice system they control to avoid punishment.

At the time, Russia was undergoing a period of restrained optimism. Dmitry Medvedev, then playing presidential understudy to Vladimir Putin, had pledged to improve the rule of law and ease political constraints. In an essay titled "Forward, Russia!" published in September 2009, Medvedev criticized the "chronic corruption" and "primitive economy" plaguing modern Russia, a state that "unfortunately combines all the shortcomings of the Soviet system with all the difficulties of contemporary life."[2] The solutions he proposed went little beyond vague calls for "modernization" and an end to a "quasi-Soviet social contract," but they encouraged many liberal-minded Russians, even if they weren't entirely sure Medvedev was the one really calling the shots. Kashin's beating was a test for Medvedev. He condemned the attacks and demanded the arrest of the assailants; later, he told Kashin he "wanted their heads torn off."[3]

For five years, nothing happened. Investigators made no arrests. No leads on the identity of the men behind the hit came through. Medvedev meekly stepped aside to let Putin return as president in 2011, prompting massive protests that Kashin helped organize. Lawmakers in the rubber-stamp parliament busily set about rolling back Medvedev's legacy, in some cases only months after having voted for parts of it. The glimmer of hope that had accompanied his presidency— *Dozhd*, a liberal news network founded during his tenure, even called itself the "optimistic channel"—flickered out as Putin cracked down on dissent, muzzled the media, ramped up nationalist sentiment, and started a war in Ukraine. As it swung firmly behind Putin, *Kommersant* forced Kashin out; he largely abandoned reporting in order to focus on opinion pieces, and moved to Switzerland, where his wife had found a job. Eduard Limonov, a legendary novelist who leads a neo-fascist opposition party, told Kashin that he and liberal Russians like him were "pale losers [with] misery written all over their faces [...] eternally doomed to defeat."[4]

Then, on September 7, 2015, Kashin wrote a post titled "Three million and three hundred thousand rubles" (about fifty thousand dollars at today's exchange rate, but double that in 2010) on his website, kashin.guru.[5] "I've known for a long time that I'd write this piece one day," he said in the post. "I just needed two names—three if you count the driver. Now I know the names." The men who beat him were Daniil Veselov and Vyacheslav Borisov, security guards at a factory in St. Petersburg. Another security guard, Mikhail Kavtaskin, had driven them there. All three were arrested. Investigators suspected Alexander Gorbunov, their boss, had organized the hit. The factory where they worked belongs to Andrei Turchak, governor of the rustic western province of Pskov. *Kommersant*, Kashin's old paper, reported that investigators believed the attack was revenge for Kashin calling the governor "fucking Turchak" and telling him to "go suck a dick" in a blog comment.[6] Turchak, astonishingly, replied hours later: "Young man, you have twenty-four hours to apologize," he commented. "The time has come."[7]

It was an extraordinary twist to the case: a sitting governor had ordered a journalist beaten half to death for a throwaway insult on a blog. But soon, things unraveled in depressingly ordinary fashion. Investigators let Gorbunov out of jail and failed to file charges against him. Nobody so much as thought to interrogate Turchak. Kashin, furious, wrote an open letter to Putin and Medvedev, excoriating them for covering it up:

You've decided to side with your Governor Turchak; you're protecting him and his gang of thugs and murderers. It would make sense for somebody like me—a victim of this gang—to be outraged about all this and tell you that it's dishonest and unjust, but I understand that such words would only make you laugh. You have complete and absolute control over the adoption and implementation of laws in Russia, and yet you still live like criminals. Every time, it's something above the law. Consider Inspector Sotskov, who's been handed my case and is now dutifully tearing it apart. Busy rescuing Turchak and his partner Gorbunov, Sotskov put it elegantly when he said recently: There's the law, but there's also the man in charge, and the will of the boss is always stronger than any law. Put bluntly: he's right and that's reality. Your will in Russia is stronger than any law, and simply obeying the law is an impossible fantasy.[8]

The scandal over Kashin's case is ongoing as I write this, and not likely to be resolved by the time this essay is published—or, indeed, after that. Nor is it likely to offer us direct insight into *Fardwor, Russia!*, which Kashin completed two months before his beating. Reading his grotesque satire of contemporary Russian life while knowing about the grotesque violence, corruption, and bureaucratic obstruction in Kashin's own, however, offers us a penetrating and unsettling picture of what Russia has become fifteen years into Putin's rule: a place where, as Kashin puts it in the same open letter, "even obvious questions about good and evil have become impossible."

Kashin's novel holds a funhouse mirror to this era, and draws heavily from the topics he wrote about while at *Kommersant*. His style is conversational and almost completely unpolished. The effect, together with the numerous references to Russian politics, history, and high and low culture, is often like reading one of his myriad columns. A notorious graphomaniac, Kashin has been known to crank out as many as eight pieces in a week, all the while tweeting prolifically, lifting language from news articles without attribution so frequently that it can be difficult to tell what is in his own voice.

("IF I WRITE BULLSHIT, IT'S A QUOTATION," he once explained.[9])

Much of the humor in the novel comes from the wry repurposing of snippets from the news. The title comes from Dmitry Medvedev's bumbling attempt to bring the Kremlin into the digital age by enthusiastically signing up for Twitter—only to misspell his own slogan in his very first tweet. An account mocking his tweets, @KermlinRussia, quickly gained hundreds of thousands of followers. The novel's basic conceit—a mystical elixir that makes midgets grow—is an obvious metaphor for the entire Medvedev era. The corrupt self-interest and wave of violence it inspires are all too familiar from contemporary Russian life. In its provincial petty criminality, the attack on the shed where the protagonist, the scientist Karpov, is experimenting on pigs, echoes the past of Turchak, who, Kashin claims, once drove around the factory shooting at stray cats from his car window. Several characters are obvious stand-ins for or composites of prominent political figures in the Medvedev era. Arkady Magomedov, the shadowy banker, gets his names from Arkady Dvorkovich, a top Medvedev aide, and the Magomedov brothers, university classmates of Dvorkovich's who rose to wealth and influence during his tenure. Close to Zero is a brazen stand-in for Vladislav Surkov, the master of the Kremlin's smoke-and-mirror politics, who once wrote a novel, *Almost Zero*, under a pseudonym. Others, like the host of the trashy chat show *Let Them Talk*, are transposed straight into the novel. Kashin rips details straight from the headlines about Olympstroi, the company accused of misusing state funds for the Sochi Olympics, and goes on for several pages.

Rewriting the realities of contemporary Russia as science fiction allows Kashin to draw out some of the era's absurdities. In genre terms, the novel is a perversion of the Soviet science fiction tradition, which told stories of heroic Soviet scientists facing down threats either from capitalists or suspiciously capitalistic alien races. The novel's plot is borrowed from *Patent AB*, a 1948 novel by Lazar Lagin, set in the fictitious capitalist country of Arzhanteiya. Steven Popf, Lagin's main character, is an idealistic young scientist who, like Karpov, comes up with an ingenious new way to make objects grow in the hope of increasing meat production. However, Popf quickly runs into resistance from Primo Padrale, Arzhanteiya's top capitalist, who wants to use his invention to monopolize the market. After Popf refuses to sell it, Padrale steals it and has Popf jailed on false murder charges. Though Arzhanteiya's communists help Popf get out of jail, he loses his laboratory and control over his invention. By changing the setting but leaving the essential details of the plot untouched, Kashin turns a didactic Soviet warning of the evils of capitalism into a comic indictment of Russian culture—where the Soviet Union itself was the greatest science fiction project of all—and the rapacious greed undercutting it. Medvedev's concept of "modernizing" Russia in top-down, Soviet-style fashion without touching the country's entrenched, retrograde bureaucracy is mocked through the concept of a "modernizational majority," a play on "Putin's majority," which his spin doctors created from the disenfranchised losers of the capitalist transition. Kashin would go on to indict the marriage of communism's Big Lie to gangster capitalism in his letter to Putin and Medvedev:

Your superstitions and your mysticism—your vision of the world that's something out of those 1980s samizdat conspiracy theories about Freemasons, and your pseudo-Russian Orthodoxy (which would have appalled Christ)—it all long ago turned you into a totalitarian sect. Most importantly, this sectarianism merged and multiplied with your old friend, the criminal ethics that ruled St. Petersburg in the 1990s. It is precisely this combination of sectarianism and gangster ideas about the nobility of absolute loyalty that make you pick Turchak, when choosing between him and the law.

Ultimately, provincial gangsterism subdues the novel's liberal characters and is revealed to pervade the entire state itself; the narrator calls it a "scum of stagnation" that envelops them all at the novel's end. "Big systems always have logistical problems," he jokes. Elena Nikolaevna, the institute director in *Fardwor, Russia!*, is only interested in Karpov's invention as a means to climb the bureaucratic ladder. The narrator describes Nikolaevna's plan as "simple: she had to have something when she went to Moscow. She didn't have that 'something,' but Karpov did. She didn't care why he was occupied with that 'something,' but it would be useful for the institute to have an idea—any idea—one that sounded good, whether or not it could be realized, something based on any sort of laboratory experiments." The other characters see Karpov's invention as a means of self-enrichment or (literal) growth, rather than a scientific contribution to society. Once the truth about the serum gets out, Medvedev's own real-life health minister, Gennady Onishchenko, is dispatched to cover it up with an absurd explanation about its real uses. The regime standing in for Medvedev's eventually exhausts itself and is swept off by the rotten core of the system it failed to improve. The narrator explains that "the project for the accelerated growth of the modernizational majority would be recognized as a mistake and would lead to some high-profile resignations in the Presidential administration and in the United Russia political party." Meanwhile, "a modernizational majority would form all by itself, and would vote in the 2012 elections for that national leader of the two whom the leaders themselves would pick in a simple game of drawing matchsticks."

Events in the Russia of real life transpired in much the same way as in *Fardwor, Russia!*, although this offers the author little solace. The novelist Vladimir Sorokin described the prophecies of his 2006 novel *Day of the Oprichnik*, in which a future Russia is ruled by an isolationist, reactionary tsar strikingly similar in rhetoric and culture to the Kremlin's inhabitants a decade after the book's publication, as a cause for despair. "Honestly, it all made me depressed. As a writer I'm satisfied, but as a citizen I'm really not," he told interviewers in 2013. "Still, there's a difference between literature and life. Fortunately," he added.[10]

For Kashin, a writer whose fiction draws so closely on real life and whose work as a reporter saw him become part of the story himself, that minimal difference offers him little protection. The most horrifying and grotesque details come from everyday life. "That's always what seemed the most interesting thing to me," Kashin wrote in the blog post exposing his attackers, describing a photograph of one of the security guards:

> Obviously, they're not people from some kind of hell; they're ordinary citizens who walk the same streets as you and me, wear shirts, eat grapes and sausage, smile for photographs, go to the movies with their girlfriends, enjoy life and consider themselves happy. I don't see anything in that photograph that would show us that he's some sort of particularly nasty person who could grab an iron bar and beat the crap out of my head fifty or so times. I still haven't understood this, so I'm going to look at that photograph some more and think (with that same head, smiley face).

Kashin's novel forces readers to confront that same problem. Is his Russian grotesque actually all that horrible? Or is the real life behind it more grotesque still?

NOTES

1 http://www.nytimes.com/2010/11/09/world/europe/09russia.html

2 http://en.kremlin.ru/events/president/news/5413

3 https://www.rt.com/politics/medvedev-wants-heads-torn/

4 https://www.facebook.com/eduard.limonov/posts/377419295711741

5 http://kashin.guru/2015/09/07/tri-milliona-trista-ty-syach-rublej/

6 http://www.kommersant.ru/doc/2805047

7 http://web.archive.org/web/20100820130424/http://kashin.livejournal.com/2795518.html?thread=20870654

8 Global Voices translated Kashin's letter into English: https://globalvoices.org/2015/10/04/a-letter-to-the-rulers-of-russia-from-oleg-kashin/

9 https://twitter.com/kshn/status/104576971538841601

10 http://www.gq.ru/magazine/featured/54702_kak_sorokin_predskazyvaet_budushchee_rossii.php

FARDWOR,
RUSSIA!

I

FOR WHATEVER REASON there were no buses waiting on the tarmac at this airport, and a line of stooping passengers, stretching to the dark concourse, was the first thing that Marina saw when they exited the plane among the last of the passengers.

"Hey, what's with you, go on," Karpov gently nudged her in the back, and Marina suddenly realized how nervous he was. "Go ahead," he repeated. "We're here."

She knew without being told that they had arrived, though the very idea of this trip still bothered her. If someone asked Marina if she knew why they had come here, she would answer without hesitation that she did not, but this would be only half the problem; after all, a wife is not required to understand everything that her husband does, sometimes it's enough to simply trust him. What bothered her more was that he himself apparently didn't understand why they'd had to give up everything in Moscow, quit their jobs, empty out their apartment, palm off their excess books and things on their friends and fly to this strange land they didn't (not even Karpov) fully understand. Karpov's anxiety frightened and upset Marina; during the flight she had almost managed to convince herself that all of her worries most likely stemmed from insecurity, whereas all that was happening was that a new life was beginning, one that was interesting but still happy like before. As for his nighttime laboratory experiments, well, they weren't exactly in a laboratory, but in the kitchen—and who the hell knows what kind of experiments they are anyway—but she always considered them a harmless hobby and of course was surprised when he suddenly told her that this hobby required sacrifices from them, like necessitating them, at the very least, to move to another city. There was nothing keeping them in Moscow, and Karpov was so convincing and, more importantly, so committed to the idea, that it didn't even occur to her to object, and she immediately agreed: yes, of course if you think so then we have to go. And although everything after that point took longer than they might have expected, they both still had plenty of time to think it over and argue about it; but for whatever reason she didn't think it over or argue, and when he told her that he had bought tickets for the twenty-eighth, she merely shrugged her shoulders—fine, the twenty-eighth, what difference does it make?

On their way to the taxi stand at this airport, he said that it probably wasn't worth the effort to head into the town now; there wouldn't be anywhere to eat dinner there and in general he didn't know if there was much of anything there at all, so it was better to spend the night in a hotel, to have dinner and breakfast in the city and to continue on to the town the next day after a good night's sleep, well-fed. For whatever reason this immediately calmed her down; if he could think about food and comfort it meant that he still had it together and could still be trusted. Having arrived at this conclusion, Marina kissed her husband silently on the cheek; Karpov flinched, and she smiled: after all these years together, he still couldn't get used to the fact that she was in constant conversation with him, even when she was silent.

They didn't bother to haggle with the taxi driver; the three hundred rubles that he wanted was perfectly acceptable. Marina got into the back, Karpov sat next to the driver, the taxi passed through a dark alley, and after a minute or so, Marina saw an illuminated crossroads bounded by a line of trees, and through the darkness behind them she could see a cemetery with crosses.

"My grandfather is buried here, and my grandmother and great-grandmother," Karpov said, and Marina for some reason thought that she was really sleepy but Karpov was still anxious, and whenever he got like this, he would always start telling stories, like now; and sure enough he started in on something about his grandfather to her or to the taxi driver, although most likely to her. She didn't really feel like listening, and just sat there smoking, smiling, and looking out the car windows at the hills interspersed with lines of trees.

She had never been in the Russian South and in general knew very little about these lands (or, in fact, about the rest of Russia either), which was typical of what seemed like every Muscovite girl from a cultured family—she had been to America, and Europe, and though she hadn't yet made it to Goa, most likely she'd get there someday; but the fate of those Russians beyond Moscow's outer beltway had passed her by; jokes about provincials and local idiots and their kind were totally foreign to her, and Karpov, though he didn't let on that he was always offended when someone would point out the inferiority of rural newcomers to the city, valued this trait in Marina too. Marina thought that he pretty much valued all of her qualities, and she smiled again.

In the meantime, the city started to appear on the hills, and Marina looked with curiosity at the fences painted in an identical blue color and the similar small one-story stone houses with rustic carved wooden trim around the windows—imitations of rural huts in unforested areas. Occasionally vacant lots appeared between the houses, and then Marina could again see the hills, now with no trees, but rather with the same kind of little houses huddling together on the hills as if Russia, even with its enormous expanses, somehow had less living space than a country like, say, crowded, tiny Holland. Then the empty spaces ended, the houses became two-storied; then there was a factory of some sort, then a round Soviet-era building, apparently a circus, and a boulevard that began after the circus. They drove down the boulevard and Karpov, gesticulating, explained something to the taxi driver. Marina liked how Karpov was able to explain things, but right now she didn't really want to figure out what he was talking about. Marina hoped that he knew what he was doing; "hoped" was the word for it.

Up to now Karpov's only argument in favor of moving out here from Moscow was that within a year he would become rich and famous, and if he didn't, then Marina had every right to leave him, get a divorce, and forget that he had ever existed. But even if this option appealed to her, she shouldn't get her hopes up, because the chance of Karpov achieving fame and fortune were one hundred percent, and after half a year she would be convinced of it.

He told her his plan in the winter, three months ago, when, having come to meet her after work, he suggested they take a walk. They stopped in a coffeehouse on Pokrovsky Boulevard to get out of the cold and warm up, and after listening to her perhaps too-detailed account of all that happened to her during the course of the day (she knew that she talked too much; she would laugh, like, you'll never be able to get a word in edgewise with me—and he would laugh too, because he was always certain that his words meant to her exactly as much as he needed to be happy), suddenly, without preface or, as in his favorite expression, "any architectural extravagances," he told her that they needed to move. Now she thought that this boulevard probably had some coffeehouses too, and Moscow seemed to no longer exist—and not even the fact that her parents remained in Moscow could convince her that earlier that same day she had been riding through Moscow from Taganka to Paveletskaya Station, where Karpov had been waiting for her with her carry-on suitcase by the ticket window for the trains to Domodedovo Airport.

Now this same suitcase was being taken out of the trunk and given to Karpov by the local taxi driver, obviously a Cossack, though this guy was nothing like some hero from *And Quiet Flows the Don* or any sort of exotic creature—he was simply a taxi driver, and that was it. For some reason Karpov had decided get out of the taxi here, several blocks from the hotel. He wanted to show Marina his favorite monument; at this point Marina could easily do without tourist excursions, but she didn't have the strength to object. A monument's a monument, after all. They walked across a wide, vast, empty space paved with enormous concrete slabs toward a precipice that offered a view of the same hills with stone huts she had seen before. At the edge of the precipice stood a gargantuan statue of a Red Army soldier in a pointed cap and trench coat; Marina had thought at first that it was made of bronze, and then realized that it was most likely a piece of tin junk. A huge foot protruded from under the overcoat (probably to keep the statue from tipping over), and behind him rose a bayonet resembling a gigantic antenna. The statue's face was deformed and not very well-designed, and its arm poked unnaturally backward. Marina could have listed another dozen absurdities of the statue's appearance, but the overall impression it produced in her was quite favorable and strong, and taking another look at the statue, Marina told Karpov (and Karpov was no longer just nervous but also noticeably embarrassed, as if he was waiting for her to tell him that she did not understand what he liked so much about this enormous piece of tin junk) that she agreed with him—this was a very, very beautiful statue indeed.

They made their way to the hotel on foot. Karpov told her that the hotel had been built by Syrian workers, and one summer, on one of his regular trips to see his grandparents, there had been a cholera outbreak in the region and his parents, who had been traveling around that summer in the Baltics, ordered his grandfather to immediately buy a ticket and bring little Karpov to them. And so while his grandfather stood in line to buy the ticket, the health services office explained that the source of the outbreak were these very Syrians, who were at first quarantined in a sanitarium and then basically thrown out of the country and sent back to their homeland once and for all, which brought the construction to an abrupt halt. The hotel stood unfinished and vacant for some fifteen years until some Chechen guy bought it. Karpov told her about the Chechen and about the Dynamo Stadium where there's a memorial plaque at the entrance honoring the Dynamo soccer team that had won the RSFSR championship back in 1949—he went on and on, displaying the fantastic volume of useless trivia that filled his head. Marina listened and suddenly realized beyond a shadow of doubt that nothing good would come of this trip, of course; Karpov's plan wouldn't succeed and she would have to return to Moscow alone—probably long before six months had passed.

II

WHEN THEY AGAIN passed the intersection by the cemetery, Karpov wasn't as nervous as he had been the day before, but something was still going on, and he even said, "No matter where or when, you really can't go home again;" and it took Marina a few extra seconds before she realized that this was actually a quote from a real poem, not just something that had come out rhyming accidentally. His mood that night infected her too. She had almost come to terms with this foreign-feeling place, with its tin Red Army soldier standing guard, but she couldn't understand what sort of place this town was where she was going to have to live, and it made her nervous.

Of course they missed their turn. They went back and forth for a long time, and then, when they had finally found their way, and Karpov had dismissed the taxi driver, they spent a while standing by the door to a building's entrance—in his childhood there hadn't been a combination lock here, but now there was, and he didn't know the code. They sat on a bench in front of the entrance; Karpov was again telling some story and Marina was again not listening, but then a tall skinny guy came out of the entrance with a bucket and Karpov got excited again, and calling out to the guy, Gennady (and using an intimate tone that was not typical of him when talking with strangers and people he didn't know well), began to explain who he was and whose grandson he was. Gennady listened silently at first, then embraced him and then, not noticing Marina, dragged Karpov into the building's entrance, and Marina followed them, then they rang and rang the doorbell of an old lady, and finally the old lady came out and also embraced Karpov and invited them for dinner, and he told her that he would come for dinner next time but that now his wife ("Oh, you're married?") was really tired, and so he needed the key. The old lady went off somewhere and then finally returned with the key, and then Karpov applied some incredible diplomatic skill in getting away, explaining to Gennady that he would drink with him next time. And only after these procedures did Marina find herself in a spacious, dusty apartment, one which had clearly been vacant for years. She went from room to room, stepped out onto the balcony, turned on the television (it worked), inspected the kitchen, then returned to the television and sat down in an armchair. She wondered whether she would like this place or not, and whether she could live here. She understood nothing. She closed her eyes.

The doorbell rang, Karpov opened it. In walked Gennady, who was evidently overjoyed at having new friends. Marina observed Gennady and Karpov through the door and decided not to get up and go into the other room. The neighbor had brought a three-liter bottle of milk and was saying something; Marina made no effort to catch what it was, but she understood that Gennady was congratulating Karpov for his wise decision: Moscow is hectic and uncomfortable, but here it's nice and quiet, and the apartment was a good one—"Warm, dry, and not a single rat."

"Well, I'm hoping to buy as much of that kind of stuff as I can here," Marina heard him say to Gennady.

"What stuff?" their neighbor didn't understand. "Apartments?"

"Not apartments," her husband laughed, "Rats, of course."

III

THE DAYS BECAME MONOTONOUS; there was absolutely nothing to do in the town, and it was quite stupid to drive to the city every day just to entertain themselves. Marina resigned herself to the fact that she wouldn't be making any friends here, and was fine with it; when you can get around the whole town in fifteen minutes, any acquaintance can mutate into an intrusive, unwanted friendship. After a week, Marina went alone to have dinner with the same neighbor who had given Karpov the keys; from their first day there, Karpov had completely withdrawn into his laboratory work, which now took place not in the kitchen, as it had in Moscow, but rather in a special shack which had also been left to him by his grandfather. He didn't invite Marina out to the shack, and she never asked to come; it wasn't so much that she didn't want to get in the way, she was afraid that she might find out her husband was placing unjustified expectations on something that was obvious folly. The neighbor, Auntie Katya Shustikova, turned out to be a sweet old lady who immediately told Marina everything she had already heard from Karpov—that at one time the town had been a military settlement, then Krushchev reduced the size of the army and then decided that agricultural science needed to be closer to the earth and, therefore, the Science Research Institute where Karpov's deceased father and his Auntie Katya's deceased husband had worked was transferred here to this boring land, and within ten years around this first building another dozen or so urban apartment buildings had popped up, entirely populated with senior and junior scientists, along with one academician from the All-Union Academy of Agricultural Science—Boris Prokopevich Goncharov, also deceased. Undoubtedly those really had been the good old days when everybody knew and loved one another, and the young obeyed their elders, and there were no drunks, and no one littered the streets; not like now, when nearly nothing remained of the institute, the bitch of a head manager was making money selling off the institute's land, the first generation of the settlement's inhabitants had died off, and now all sorts of outsiders living in the buildings had no clue about all of this good magic that now remained only in the form of Auntie Katya's fond memories.

Auntie Katya, of course, was also interested in what Karpov was going to be doing, and when Marina answered that she herself didn't know for sure, the old lady, of course, didn't believe her, but she didn't let on and instead talked about how Karpov's grandfather had once been involved with something very mysterious—"petroleum growth substance," which had actually been extracted from oil by a bunch of fraudulent Azeri Lysenkoist scientists, and his grandfather had really thought that if this petroleum product were fed to pigs then the pigs would put on weight faster than if they were fed normal food. But the pigs had a natural "human" reaction to the oil—they refused to eat it, and force-feeding led to massive deaths; and then Lysenko's genetics project went out of fashion, the program was canceled, and Karpov's grandfather, having come to terms with the fact that his career had been a failure, worked until retirement at the institute's Department of Propaganda and Agitation, nursing a hatred for agriculture and any other science in any shape or form.

This cautionary tale certainly didn't make Marina any more optimistic, and that evening, when Karpov returned from his shack, she demanded that her husband tell her, sparing no detail, what exactly he was up to and what was fueling his dreams of fame and fortune. Karpov was unexpectedly eager to explain it—Marina even related his lecture to me, but I, having only the vaguest notion about scientific terminology, am not going to risk a game of garbled "telephone" by trying to summarize Karpov's explanations here. I will only say that Karpov is definitely not a biologist, nor a chemist, or even a pharmacist by education, but back in Moscow he had invented some kind of serum which, when injected into living creatures, would increase their growth potential many times; the rats, which the kind Gennady had trapped for a little money at Karpov's request, had already grown to the size of large sheepdogs, and Karpov had begun serious efforts to kill them using an electric shock, because he had still not figured out how to get the test animals to stop growing once they reached the desired size, but all the same he would figure it out, and when he did he would be able to open his own business, which would bring their family the fortune they had come here to seek. Karpov burned the dead rats in a special vat, but he skinned the fur off to then stuff them, and he could even show Marina these hides, though he doubted that she would appreciate the sight. Sure enough, she refused to go and look at the rat hides; but her husband's story, though it was entirely convincing, for some reason didn't calm her—she already realized what she would dream about that night, and the prospect of seeing gigantic rats in her dreams quite understandably frightened her. As she lay in bed, she wanted to tell her husband, "Let's just leave," but Karpov was already asleep, and she couldn't bring herself to wake him.

She dreamed that night, but not about rats. She dreamed of Karpov's funeral in an old cemetery (might it be the same cemetery they had passed twice?), and she was there—young, as she was now, but somehow very different, a stranger to herself. She had been afraid to awaken Karpov, but he woke her up and showed her that her pillow was wet—it seems that she had been crying in her sleep. While Marina was thinking up something to say to her husband about the source of these tears, Karpov fell asleep. Marina wiped away her tears and fell back asleep herself, this time without any dreams.

IV

IN THE MORNING the doorbell rang; Marina opened the
door. Just as on their first day there, Gennady had come
over with some milk. From Auntie Katya, Marina had
learned that Gennady was a war veteran on a pension;
his parents had lived here, and when he retired from the
army, unmarried and good-for-nothing, he moved back
to live with them in 1991. His parents died shortly thereafter, and now Gennady lived alone raising chickens and,
more importantly, serving as a kind of keeper of the local
traditions which had almost completely died out. He con-
tributed to the spread of news and gossip throughout the
town, showed visitors the ropes—the way things were done
around here—giving instructions to teenagers and drivers
parking improperly—in general, he kept the town from

turning into a random collection of suburban five-story, Soviet apartment buildings in the middle of the steppe.

For example, this time he had brought not only milk but also an important communication: the director of the institute, an associate member of the Russian Academy of Natural Sciences, Elena Nikolaevna Gorskaya, whose birthday was today, would be pleased to see Mr. Karpov and his wife at her party that night; even though she couldn't remember Karpov's grandfather, she had no doubt that his grandson was a fine man who would undoubtedly become a friend of all the employees at the institute.

When Marina relayed this message to her husband, he immediately said that he would not be going to any birthday party, that he was planning an important experiment, and he was not about to sacrifice it for the sake of a bunch of strangers who just wanted to gawk at him. But Marina explained to Karpov that he was an idiot and if he wanted to live here for even a month, then he had to build the right relationships with the locals, both the local dignitaries as well as ordinary people, and if they want to see him, he should meet them halfway, or else they would point the finger at him. For some reason this argument about "pointing the finger" impressed Karpov; he wearily asked if he needed to put on a suit, and Marina began to laugh; in short, the incident was settled.

The path that led from their home to the institute was paved with yellow coquina shell and lined on the left and the right with blue spruce trees planted by the Regional Committee, which indicated that at one time everything at the institute had been well and good. The path was no more than a hundred meters long, it took just a minute and a half to walk it, but the Karpovs, of course, were late all the same. Marina was certain that it was her husband's fault: he had taken forever in the shower washing off the rat smell; while Karpov thought that Marina had taken too long putting on her make-up. Despite that, neither husband nor wife was mad at the other because, for all intents and purposes, who would care if they were late to a voluntary gathering? It's not like it's a plane to catch, after all.

When they walked into the assembly hall of the institute, from the stage of which a fat man in glasses was reading a speech on the scientific achievements of the esteemed Elena Nikolaevna (listening to the mumbling of the fat man, Karpov quickly realized that the director had not achieved anything of particular merit), the audience in the hall— people who clearly knew each other well and had for a long time—of course, immediately shifted their attention to the couple, and Marina felt uncomfortable under the gazes of a hundred and fifty pairs of eyes, with every pair attached to a mouth suffering from a lack of gossip. Marina knew that the next day kind Gennady would tell her everything that the institute's women thought about her dress and her hair, and Karpov, apparently, also felt something similar, because at one point he took his wife's hand and gave it a little squeeze, as if to say, "Don't worry."

Meanwhile, the fat man relinquished his place on the stage to a Cossack choir which apparently consisted of scientists from the institute, because the caps and tunics they wore did not necessarily go very well with the bespectacled countenances of the singing men, and plus their out-of-tune singing indicated that these Cossacks hadn't learned to sing at home but rather from going to see a national festival of historical song and dance. They sang to Elena Nikolaevna's health, but the only phrase distinguishable in their song was her name, which was repeated obsessively in the chorus. The audience clapped more enthusiastically for the Cossacks than for the speaker, who, as Marina had already learned from a conversation between two women sitting behind her, was named Vyacheslav Kirillovich, and he headed up not just any department, but nanotechnology, which in its turn served as a sign of the institute's progressive nature and its director in particular.

The fact that Elena Nikolaevna was a progressive and modern woman became apparent to Karpov at the banquet in the winter garden after the ceremonial part of the evening (naturally, not everyone was invited, but the Karpovs were dragged there—"You absolutely must!"—by a pretty young blonde girl with huge fake nails—probably a secretary). Not knowing anybody, Karpov and Marina felt uncomfortable and saved themselves by relating some banal tales of life in Moscow, of which they had a lot that they hadn't shared with anybody before; their stories were of the types of thing that were commonplace in Moscow, but in this winter garden it all sounded like stories of extraterrestrial life; and Marina, who still hadn't made up her mind whether she liked being an extraterrestrial, reminisced to her husband about Moscow's taxi drivers and waitresses, colleagues and superiors, about some people she knew who were unfamiliar to Karpov, and even he began to miss that city from which had been so eager to escape just two weeks prior.

Most likely, they could have just slipped away without being noticed, but the evening's honoree came up to them;

she was a woman in her fifties, also a blonde, but whose hair, unlike the other blonde's, was obviously bleached. They had not seen her in the assembly during the festivities, but here it was somehow immediately apparent to them that she was the most important person in town. Elena Nikolaevna was holding two glasses of champagne. She gave them to Marina and Karpov, leaving herself empty-handed; Karpov undertook to go get her some champagne, but Elena Nikolaevna followed him, and he somehow understood that this whole invitation had been contrived precisely for this moment, for an important and sensitive conversation, and that now he would be hearing something that, though not really of any importance to him, would nevertheless unpleasantly complicate his life.

And so, as he handed a glass of champagne to the director, he himself initiated the conversation—he said that in his childhood, walking around the institute with his grandmother, he had understood that the most awe-inspiring people in the world worked right here in this very building, and that he was now very glad to meet the person in charge of all these awe-inspiring people. In his improvisation, Karpov hadn't been able to come up with precisely what made those people so inspiring, so he cleverly changed the subject to a touching reminiscence: by the main entrance to the institute, there had been a display board with a sign reading: "Best People," and once, he, only five years old at the time, had cried because he hadn't found his grandfather on the board (who, of course, was the best person ever), and he stopped crying only when his grandmother took him inside the building and showed him another board with photos of war veterans, among whom he saw his grandfather. Afterward, as Karpov found out years later, his grandmother had gone to see Professor Pilipenko, the now-deceased former director of the institute, and she had talked him into replacing the "Best People" sign that was traumatizing for little kids with a neutral "Board of Honor." Elena Nikolaevna laughed politely—politely enough for Karpov to understand that he wouldn't succeed in small-talking this woman, and, all right then, he would just have to listen to whatever it was that had made her drag him here in the first place.

Elena Nikolaevna started out in general terms. She asked whether Karpov had liked the speech, and, before he could answer, she started talking about Vyacheslav Kirillovich, who, since he had graduated from the Russian State Agricultural University, was not at all familiar with cutting-edge nanotechnologies. She had a problem; all of her correspondence with the Russian Nanotechnology Corporation had to do with the fact that her institute didn't have a single project, not even any crazy idea that could attract the interest of the corporation that could lead to a source of revenue. That's why, starting the next month, Vyacheslav Kirillovich's job title would become more promising—"Deputy Director for Innovations"—and she, as the director, would go to Moscow and start searching for a source of big money in different places; at the current time, innovation was in fashion, and Elena Nikolaevna had the power of persuasion.

"I have a talent for persuasion," she repeated, "but, alas, not for generating ideas. And you can understand how glad I was to learn that a mysterious genius had shown up in our little town, and had gone ahead and built himself a laboratory and begun doing some kind of brilliant research all by himself without even asking me for any help."

Karpov had never been called a man of genius, not even by Marina, and though he ought to have been embarrassed by what she said, for some reason he wasn't—it was clear to him that in the time he'd been here, the talkative Gennady had managed to tell everyone that Karpov was doing some kind of experiments on rats in his shack; but Gennady couldn't fathom the nature of those experiments, therefore Elena Nikolaevna couldn't either; and if that were so, then why would she compliment him? Karpov raised his glass for a toast, and said that he was very flattered by praise from such a distinguished person, which he, of course, considered Elena Nikolaevna to be, but he could not understand what she was getting at. They clinked glasses. The director gulped down the champagne like vodka, with a grimace. She smiled:

"I really have no idea what you are doing in there with those rats. It's fine, do whatever you'd like, even clone them. I can offer you a position as a senior research associate and a proposition—I will be your..."

"Censor?" Karpov recalled such a moment from Pushkin's life, but he already understood where the director was heading.

"No, not your censor," Elena Nikolaevna smiled once again. "Your co-author."

Her plan was simple: she had to have something when she went to Moscow. She didn't have that "something," but Karpov did. She didn't care why he was occupied with that "something," but it would be useful for the institute to have an idea—any idea—one that sounded good, whether or not it could be realized, something based on any sort of laboratory experiments. And if she was to be completely honest, the institute had not been doing any scientific work for some time now; instead it had been earning cash by renting out its facilities and land—this gave a steady income, but it was not all that much. But there was big money lying around these days and at that very moment important people in Moscow were determining which establishments to include in a federal target program called "A Well-Fed Russia," whose mission was to foster innovative technologies in agriculture. There are many agricultural institutes in Russia, and it would be a shame if some slackers from Belgorod or Krasnodar were to get their hands on the government's millions; because obviously if anyone deserved the money, it was this institute, the one to which Karpov's deceased granddad had dedicated years of his selfless labor. Karpov didn't understand what his grandfather had to do with it, but he nodded anyway.

"I'm so glad that you agree," Elena Nikolaevna whispered fervently. She had already come up with a plan: the next morning Karpov would bring her a description of his work, she would stamp the institute's seal of approval on it and fly off to Moscow to get the money. Of course she would have to give almost half of it to the official in the ministry in charge of the allotment of funds for the program, but Karpov shouldn't worry—there would be lots of money, enough for everyone, including him.

Karpov understood about half of what the director was saying. What he did clearly understand was that it had to do with some sort of corrupt scheme; it didn't really bother him that Elena Nikolaevna was hoping to use his help to rob the state; he had no warm feelings for it anyway, and he wouldn't even object to this state money going to this particular woman—if it didn't go to her, someone else would steal it all the same. But the co-authoring proposition had really offended him for some reason. He had no doubts of his invention's future success, and being a conceited person by nature, for a long time he had pictured himself—if, of course, not as a Nobel Prize-winner (after all, he wasn't even a scientist, but rather, just an amateur inventor), at least someone who would appear on the front-page of all the world's major newspapers. And when he pictured this woman by his side on the front page, he got really angry. He wanted to be polite and say that he would definitely think over her enticing offer, but instead, he grumbled, perhaps more rudely than he should have: "No, I am not interested in your offer," turned, and walked away.

Marina was all too happy that they got out of there so quickly—while Karpov had been chatting with Elena Nikolaevna, she had been accosted by some agronomist lady who was for some reason particularly interested in whether Karpov was a faithful husband. Marina answered that yes, he was, but the woman's obtrusiveness had spoiled her mood.

V

KARPOV KEPT DISAPPEARING into his shack from morning to night, and Marina had already gotten used to having no entertainment except for television and the Internet (yes, she herself had called the cable guy, who had come from a local provider and set up cable Internet in their apartment), since it didn't look like any more options were about to become available. But one day Karpov came in from the shack around 5:00 p.m. in an excessively good mood and bearing a bottle of champagne. Marina immediately knew that something important and good had happened and, hopefully, since this important and good thing had happened, they could finally return to Moscow and Karpov would become rich and famous, and she would be the wife of "the one and only Karpov," which suited her just fine; for as had been written, "The great man stared through the window, but her entire world ended with the border of his broad Greek tunic."

But it turned out that all the fuss just about some small victory that didn't affect Marina's life at all—Karpov had finally managed to regulate his serum so that once his test rats reached adult size they would stop growing before they turned into enormous monsters.

"What now?" Marina asked.

"Now..." her husband paused in thought. "Now I need a midget."

Of course, experiments on people in Russia are forbidden by law, as in any civilized country, but Karpov didn't see this as an obstacle to performing a miracle, and turning a midget into a normally-sized person, of course, can be considered a real miracle, and as long as Marina didn't rat out Karpov to the cops, then she needn't be afraid of anything—no one would find out how the test midget grew, and the midget himself would be happy. They got online and started scouring the Internet for midgets, and within a minute, on some local message-board for young parents, they found a fascinating discussion about a new show at the city circus—all those young parents without exception advised one another not to bring their children to this new show under any circumstances, because there was no spectacle more sad and boring. The clowns weren't funny, the trained cows and cats were boring, and most shameful of all was the midget Vasya, who did impersonations of popular Norwegian singer Alexander Rybak, but the way he performed them made you wish he'd never done them in the first place.

Karpov immediately called the circus and found out that the next show would take place the next day.

"Shall we go meet Vasya?" he asked Marina. Marina kissed her husband—she had wanted to go to the city with Karpov for some fun for some time now.

VI

THEY MADE A POINT of coming to the city early to have dinner in a restaurant and stroll along the boulevard before the show. Karpov brought his wife to the tin Red Army soldier again, but this time its shape didn't impress Marina at all; it was just a statue like any other. She had been in a bad mood pretty much all day, and she knew why: when Karpov spoke, what he said seemed logical and proper to her, but when he was silent, and she allowed herself to think about it, then all her husband's ingenious ideas started to seem if not dubious, then at least peculiar. An experiment on a living person—what if it goes wrong; what if the midget grows into a twenty-meter giant and destroys the city; and what if Karpov gets thrown in jail? Or even without the giant, what if the midget is insulted by Karpov's dangerous proposal, and he calls the cops and Karpov gets into some kind of mess?

Going to the circus itself, however, was one big mess—quality obviously did not appear to be a priority for the circus, and Marina even asked Karpov to let her go somewhere and wait for him on neutral territory. Karpov didn't mind, and Marina probably would have even gone, but she suddenly felt sorry for her husband. She stayed and watched as a hung-over clown in the ring hit a cow on the horns with a balloon hammer, while the cow, advertised on the circus poster as an erudite animal in the sense that it could count, mournfully mooed as many times as the hammer hit her horns. Then some Krasnolozhkin performed—on the posters he was advertised as a student of the great cat-trainer Yuri Kuklachev and, probably, he really was, because this Krasnolozhkin's skinny cats so desperately tried to act like trained ones, and they were so pitiful that Marina probably would have again asked to go to some café if Karpov hadn't looked so pleadingly—he himself, of course, shared his wife's feelings for the circus, but unlike her, he was prepared to do anything just to make it to the moment the midget Vasya would come out.

Vasya, when he appeared, did not deviate from the show's general format—he was a bit cuter than the cats and a bit more pathetic than the cow. In contrast to the animals, however, he was his own trainer and master of ceremonies—he galloped on a pony, shot a miniature gun at plates thrown into the air by an assistant (twice, of course, he missed), but then jumped with surprising grace from his little pony, pulled out of somewhere a tiny, probably plastic, violin, and, accompanying himself, began to sing in a horrid child's voice: "Years ago, when I was younger, I kinda liked a girl I knew, she was mine and we were sweethearts, that was then but then it's true." If Marina found out that the lyrics had been written by Vasya himself she wouldn't have been surprised—the midget himself and his violin, along with his voice and the song, came together remarkably well as a cohesive composition—and it was simply impossible to determine which of those distinct parts was the most offensive.

Marina glanced over at her husband—Karpov looked like the happiest man on Earth. Obviously if he could, he would have been happy to gobble this little Vasya up whole, but since Karpov's range of morally acceptable activities didn't include cannibalism, he limited himself to passing

OLEG KASHIN

a note to the midget through a manager. It read something like, "Blah blah blah, I'm Karpov from Moscow, I would like to talk to you about a very important matter, I'm waiting for you in such and such coffee shop across the street from the circus."

While they sat and waited for Vasya in the coffee shop, Marina told Karpov several times that Vasya, of course, would not come, because being a midget in the circus not only entailed riding a pony around the arena, but also drinking oneself silly after the show, and if Karpov couldn't understand that, then that was just proof of his ignorance. Karpov disagreed halfheartedly, but Marina saw that her husband was starting to get nervous again—the chances of not seeing Vasya were very high. And perhaps that's why, when the midget did actually appear, Karpov's face lit up with a degree of joy only possible for a twenty-nine-year-old married man without children and a proper job.

For his part, Vasya, as quickly became apparent, was for some reason certain that Karpov was not only from Moscow, but from the Nikulin Circus on Tsvetnoy Boulevard; and so, when it became apparent that no one was going to try to lure him to Moscow, the midget became bored and started to display a willingness to leave, especially since Karpov nearly ruined everything—without any preliminaries, he told the midget that he wanted to "make him a bit taller." It's well known that midgets are very sensitive to even the slightest joke about their anthropometrical statistics, and the fact that Vasya didn't start a brawl with Karpov right away, if it meant anything, meant only that Vasya had some self-esteem issues. In any case, the conversation began to take on a hostile tone, and Marina realized that she needed to get involved. She took Vasya by the hand and very calmly began to explain to him that her husband didn't mean any harm, and that though Marina herself didn't understand how, he really was going to try to make Vasya taller.

They talked for a long time. Then they were silent. Karpov tore a piece of paper from his notebook and wrote down a list of foods that Vasya needed to eat after the injection. Then Vasya and Karpov went into the bathroom together, and though Marina couldn't see Karpov massage the rubbing alcohol onto Vasya's arm and jab a syringe half-full of yellowish liquid into his vein, he really did, honest.

When Karpov and the midget came out of the bathroom, the barmaid gave them a judgmental look. After all, the south has always been the most conservative part of the country.

VII

AND IT'S PROBABLY for the best that right after that trip to the city Karpov became violently ill—he caught a cold, didn't tend to it, and was bedridden with pneumonia for three days. And if he hadn't become bedridden, he probably would have distracted us from following the fate of the midget Vasya, which was, without a doubt, worth following.

At first no one noticed anything—Vasya still rode his pony every night, playing his violin, singing his stupid song. You couldn't tell his height—ninety-three centimeters or, let's say, ninety-five centimeters—from afar. They say that it's the same with pregnant women: you look at her—she seems the same as usual, just like yesterday, and then just like that—a huge stomach; how did it happen?

The same thing happened with Vasya. He went on riding his pony every night, but then one night a military man in the audience, pretending that he was speaking only to his female companion, but loud enough for everyone to hear, said: "In my unit, we have about two hundred midgets like him, but they're even shorter than this guy," and he tacked on a few swear words. Vasya, of course, didn't fall from his pony, but he was upset—as of that morning his height had grown already to 121 cm, while yesterday it was 119 cm, and how tall he would be the next day he could only guess.

But height wasn't the whole problem, people had just laughed at the military blabbermouth and forgotten about it by the next day; but what to do with his voice? It had cost Vasya a lot of effort over the past few days to maintain his childish tenor when he sang. You might have assumed that with every centimeter gained in height, his voice would crack like a teenager's, but Vasya hadn't thought of this, and Karpov hadn't mentioned it. Taking his last turn around the ring on his pony, Vasya thought that he had a right to be furious at Karpov, but he couldn't make himself be furious, because even though his circus career was right there and then going up his pony's ass, the transformation itself, which the midget was going through, exhilarated him. But not even that was enough—the word "exhilarated" used to describe this miracle would sound offensive. Generally speaking, Vasya didn't have the most impressive vocabulary, and the midget knew that, but he also knew that there are no such words in Russian or any other language that could describe what was actually happening to him.

But it's Vasya we're talking about here, a pathetic circus midget, who couldn't even remember his parents, or who it was who had taught him to drink or when that happened, or even how he had ended up in the circus after leaving the orphanage. As for me, I have a much richer vocabulary than this midget, therefore, I, unlike him, can say exactly what was happening to him—a downfall. Yes, a horrible downfall at that moment when he, having jumped off the pony, took out his violin and started singing the Rybak song about loving and fighting with his girl in a voice even more wretched than the night Karpov first saw him—hoarse, and nearly masculine.

To provoke jeering and booing in such a circus is in itself a kind of heroic deed, and the day when the audience's jeers and shouts drove Vasya back behind the curtain may very well have been the most important day in the history of this particular cultural institution. When the noise behind his back had stopped, Vasya, walking along by the pathetic trained cow's cage, suddenly realized that he had never been so happy, and the dumb, happy expression on his face lingered even in the office of the circus director, who had decided to stay at work that night later than usual in order to wrap up some unfinished business (and there will be a lot more unfortunate coincidences in this story). He did not lack intelligence, this Sergei Nikolaevich Kozlov, director of the municipal cultural institution, the City Circus. He clearly understood the artistic value of the troupe entrusted to him, and he even felt sincerely sorry for those people, especially children, who for some mysterious reason came to the circus seeking entertainment. Sergei Nikolaevich didn't have any illusions, and he generally valued his position for the opportunity it gave him to rent out the circus facilities and to run his own personal gambling parlor with slot machines in the basement of the building. When gambling was banned by the government and he had to order a new sign for the gambling parlor, "Internet-Café," the trained cow had gone without decent food for a month, and Sergei Nikolaevich felt sorry for the cow too.

In general, he was not only smart, but he could be kind; but when Vasya entered his office that night, Sergei

Nikolaevich took a minute to decide what kind of person he should be that day: smart or kind. If he was to be kind, that meant he would also have be curious and sympathetic, and then he would, of course, have to ask the midget what had happened to him and why he had grown so much in the last few days. But that's if he was kind; the smart person inside Sergei Nikolaevich sighed and immediately came to the conclusion that such a tall midget would not be able to amaze the audience anymore. Not that Sergei Nikolaevich was so concerned with profits from the circus—no, he was just afraid of scandal, because any scandal could end up drawing unwelcome attention from the municipal cultural department, which was fully capable of sending a new director into this office, forcing Sergei Nikolaevich into early retirement.

All the inner turmoil between the smart Sergei Nikolaevich and the kind Sergei Nikolaevich took no more than a minute to play itself out—plenty of time to erase the happy smile from Vasya's face, giving him time to prepare himself psychologically for whatever the director might ask him. And the question, when it came, was quite philosophical and rhetorical:

"So what the fuck is up with you growing?"

Sergei Nikolaevich didn't really care about the answer. He didn't even care about the circumstances surrounding Vasya's growth and the fact that he was still growing (and this was the question that Vasya feared the most, because Karpov had asked him not to tell anyone about the injection, and the midget hadn't yet come up with an alternative explanation for his growth). His only concern was whether or not Vasya understood that if "Clown (Midget)" was written on his professional résumé, then he needed to remain a midget, and if he didn't want to remain a midget, then why the hell was he still working in the circus? Having expressed this basically simple and correct idea to Vasya, Sergei Nikolaevich announced that he was officially letting him go, and that Vasya need not come in to work the next day.

Of course Vasya had expected something like this, and so he was surprised at himself that instead of a simple "Thank you" or some sort of rude reply, he said that he wouldn't let it end like this and that he would be suing Sergei Nikolaevich and his circus. Most likely, Karpov's injection not only made arms and legs grow, but also his self-esteem, or something like that. And, of course, Karpov hadn't warned Vasya about this either.

VIII

OF COURSE, the news wasn't front-page material (or as they say, "a cover story"), and no one had claimed that it would be; it was just a funny little blurb: midget sues circus that fired him for growing taller. They had their laugh, of course, decided to report it, then switched to other topics—something about Lyudmila Gurchenko. The first day the news appeared on the paper's website along with a video clip, and the next day it came out in the paper itself—a quarter-pager with the headline, "Growing Pains" (the editor replaced the phrase "Vasya couldn't hold back his tears" with "'I'm simply shocked,' Vasya told our correspondent"). And then the day after that a girl of an indeterminate age showed up at the courthouse and introduced herself to Vasya, but he didn't catch her name. She said that she worked for Channel One as the special editor of guest selection for the television program *Let Them Talk*, and she asked if Vasya wanted to earn a little money (three hundred dollars, as he learned later) and go to Moscow for a couple days to be on the show and, well, to become famous, because he must have always wanted to become famous, or else why would he have ever wanted to work for the circus? Vasya didn't really listen to what the girl was saying—he was far more interested in picturing her naked; for some reason, as of late he had been imagining all the women he met with no clothes on, and his palms had started getting sweaty on a regular basis. To Moscow? Why not? He had heard of *Let Them Talk* before, and though he wasn't all that eager to appear on television, he really would love to go to Moscow ("A change of scenery," Vasya thought to himself); he had never been there before. Before six the next morning the girl ordered a taxi to go to the building where Vasya lived; he walked out of the building's archway—a normal-sized guy, not tall, really, but no midget either, and the editor even thought that the show's host Andrei Malakhov might not even believe that Vasya had ever been a midget. They rode in silence, and in half an hour they were at the airport.

The flight to Moscow took an hour and forty minutes. Vasya, as it turned out, had never flown before, and the editor (we call her a girl, but she was really forty-two, named Inna, divorced, with a thirteen-year-old daughter, Olesya) was even worried that Vasya might get sick on takeoff, but the ex-midget fell asleep while the plane was still on the ground, with his head on her shoulder, and she looked at him and for some reason also imagined him with no clothes on. Jumping ahead, just to let you know, that same night in Moscow, in a room at the Altai Hotel, Inna would become the first woman in Vasya's life, and Vasya would become her first man in the last year and a half. Love is basically amazing, when you get down to it.

IX

INNA, BY THE WAY, didn't have to worry—she could have been equally successful at dragging any type of person to the show's taping, because during the whole time he was on the program, Vasya only managed to get out one sentence, "I was unjustly fired;" the host Malakhov told the rest of the story for him. Malakhov had a folder with an article printed off the Internet in it, "Growing Pains." There were lots of people in the studio along with Vasya: an actor from a popular court drama, the famous cat trainer Yuri Kuklachev; a State Duma representative from the party United Russia (his name and face Vasya couldn't remember later); and some other people, including the film director Sergei Soloviev; whom Malakhov tried to remind several times that he had midgets in the cast of his movie *Assa*,

OLEG KASHIN

but Soloviev kept talking about *Anna Karenina* instead. If
Karpov were a TV watcher, he would probably have been
disappointed—if not about the general idiocy of the discussion, then at least because Vasya didn't call him after his
growth spurt. But Karpov didn't watch television and he still
hadn't fully recovered from his illness—he didn't go to his
shack, but lay on the sofa talking to Marina, who, although
she enjoyed listening to Karpov's childhood stories, could
hardly conceal the fact that she didn't like living there and
that she would be all too happy if Karpov agreed that it was
time to move back to Moscow.

But the fact that the Karpovs don't watch television
doesn't mean that nobody watches television. The show
wasn't even over when the phone rang in the office of
Let Them Talk; it was the secretary of the Vremya-Kapital
corporation, and she wanted to know if that midget they
were showing on TV was still in Moscow. In fact Vasya
might have already left, because the filming had taken
place the day before, but Inna had changed his ticket and
paid for the hotel room for another twenty-four hours—
she would have paid for another couple of days, but she
didn't have the funds. What the Vremya-Kapital corporation needed with Vasya the secretary didn't say, but half

an hour later a taxi stopped by the hotel Altai and within ten minutes Inna was left all by herself in the room, while Vasya, escorted by a silent security guy with a shaved head, was on Altufievskoe Highway in the taxi, heading for the Moscow Beltway.

I guess it's time to tell you about who Vremya-Kapital really are (well, you understand that the name of the corporation has been changed; unlike Vasya, I don't want to have to go to court). In Russia there are a number of companies whose names are not bandied about, and they get in the news much less frequently than Gazprom or Lukoil, but if you take a closer look, they have their assets in the oil and gas industries, metal-working, telecommunications, construction; and the name of the owner, though not as familiar to the public as, say, "Roman Abramovich," firmly maintains an honorable position somewhere between fifteenth and twenty-fourth place in the Russian *Forbes'* annual list of billionaires.

The founder of Vremya-Kapital, Arkady Magomedovich Magomedov, it must be said, had made it in to *Forbes* just once—in 2004—and back then the editor hadn't been able to find a photo of him, and instead of a photo portrait, they had published a shaded silhouette (rumors were that the deceased Paul Klebnikov fined one of the staff for this failure).

Not much was known about Arkady Magomedovich. He was born somewhere between Dagestan and Georgia, spent time in prison for something or other from 1982 to 1986. By the way, when he was in prison, David Tukhmanov wrote a song especially for Magomedov, "In My House," to make his experience in the big house more pleasant; it was first performed by Sofia Rotaru at a concert on Soviet Police Day in 1983—later Magomedov would give Tukhmanov a cherry-red Mercedes-Benz for this gesture. After he was released, he immediately became a well-known figure in the cooperative business movement; the co-op youth respectfully called him an old *tsekhovik*, but we have no further details about him. December 6, 1999 is considered the date of the founding of the Vremya-Kapital corporation; Vremya was the name of a chain of video salons in Moscow train stations founded by Arkady Magomedovich in 1988 and which remained in business until 1992. Under this nostalgic brand-name, he consolidated all of his assets and in 2003, when the offices of Vremya were raided, there was even an article in *Kommersant* with the headline, "They Came for Magomedov." They came but walked away with nothing, everything went back to normal. Wagging tongues say that Magomedov managed to get a call through to the president's right-hand man, Igor Sechin, and explained to him that the most influential clans of Chechnya, Ingushetia, and Dagestan, which had business relations with Magomedov, were ready to do everything they could to destabilize the situation in the north Caucasus if Arkady Magomedov's businesses were to be subjected to so much as a threat from the government. Whether or not Sechin took this seriously is not known. After several days, the vice president of Vremya was kidnapped, held for a week at someone's country house, apparently in Serebryany Bor (Kukushkin could see a church on the other side of the river), and was fed some pills that were meant to loosen up his tongue. With his loosened tongue, Kukushkin told them that, yes, if Magomedov were to go to jail, there would be war in the Caucasus—but he had nothing more to say, that's all he knew. After that Kukushkin would be found sleeping in a subway car at the Vykhino metro station, he would then retire from his position as vice-president and move to America on a pension supplied by Magomedov.

After Kukushkin's kidnapping, Vremya was left alone, and from this point forward Vremya became especially aggressive on the market; it is known that at one point there was an incident, for example, with the director of one of the oil refineries in western Siberia who wasn't happy with the amount of compensation that Magomedov offered him for a controlling share in the factory. Someone higher up in Moscow even offered the director protection, and he was going to go to talk about Magomedov with that important someone, but he didn't make it to Moscow—on the way to the airport he told the driver he wanted to go for a swim before his flight (in September, in the Irtysh River!), so he ran to the river, throwing his clothes off along the way, jumped in, and died of a heart attack in the water. What it all meant, no one really knew, but all the other business owners whose companies were of interest to Vremya, when they retell this story to each other have since that time preferred not to contradict Magomedov. And when Magomedov suddenly died in 2005, it seemed like the entire *Forbes* list and half of the presidential administration flew in to Derbent for his funeral.

The funeral procession was headed up by his eldest son—one of the deceased's two heirs—Kirill Arkadievich (they interred Magomedov "Russian-style," on the third day, in a coffin without a mufti; whether or not he was

actually a Muslim, nobody knew). Arkady Magomedov had
left his fortune to his two sons, but the youngest, Mefody,
didn't come to the funeral, he didn't appear in public at all
during these years, although, along with Kirill, he was the
"co-chairman of the board of directors"—a one-of-a-kind
job title in world business practices, it turns out. Vremya's
public relations office explained that all the representative
functions had been taken over by Kirill Magomedov, and
Mefody Arkadievich became the brains of the corporation, and that it was he who did all of Vremya's strategic
planning. A source from *Vedomosti* remarked that it was
this Mefody Magomedov who was responsible for all of
Vremya's major contracts, and without his younger brother
Kirill would not have been able to hold together the empire
left by their father.

In reality, of course, that's not at all how things really
were; and if Kirill, catching up on his sleep on flights
between Hong Kong and London and blushing before
Prime Minister Putin at glitzy crisis management meetings,
carried the whole business on his shoulders, then Mefody
was a clueless and selfish rich slacker who would spend
half the year traveling around far-off countries (Bhutan,
Nepal, all the way to Colombia) and the other half sitting

around in his personal castle in the village of Barvikha in the Odintsovsky region of Moscow Oblast. Mefody would most likely have been deserving of more than a few of the dirtiest curses, if not for one convincing reason, which he, of course, possessed, and which Vasya encountered when the security guard delivered him to Mefody's castle and, having opened the door into an enormous study, left him alone in the dimly lit chamber.

The study was empty, or so it seemed to Vasya. On the walls hung two paintings—a portrait of a gloomy Caucasian with graying temples, dressed in royal robes (Vasya can be forgiven for not recognizing either the late Arkady Magomedovich or the brush of Ilya Glazunov) and a black square in a glass frame. At the end of the study stood a table with no one behind it, and Vasya took a step forward, assuming as he approached the table that somebody would surely be coming in; but the moment the former midget took his first step, a squeaky voice greeted him from somewhere off to his right. Vasya turned his head and saw a couch with an unpleasant-looking midget in a silk dressing gown reclining on it.

"Hello Vasya," the midget said. "Not a centimeter over ninety," Vasya thought to himself as he returned the greeting.

X

ARKADY MAGOMEDOV was buried in the godless Russian style for a good reason. He had tried to determine his relationship with God many times (both in jail and after), but the only thing he understood was that he had already received his punishment in the form of his son, the freak, therefore he had nothing else to worry about. He loved Mefody very much, and Kirill (there was a two years' difference between the sons) knew from a very early age that because his younger brother was not growing, anyone who offended him was an enemy, and Mefody himself was near and dear, and whatever happened later in life, Kirill needed to do everything that he could to ensure that his brother would never doubt his own integrity as a human being for a second.

They were abroad when the news about their father's death reached them; both were in America: Kirill in Boston, Mefody in Miami. That only one brother would go back for the funeral was never called into question, but Kirill felt uneasy when, talking on the phone with Mefody, instead of the proper words of condolence, the first thing his brother asked was how to say in English, "*Za moi zhe pryaniki ya eshche i pidoras.*" While Kirill was on the plane from Boston to Makhachkala, he was wondering whether his brother would want to split up the company, contrary to their father's last wishes—in principle, finding himself some strong allies somewhere in the corridors of the Kremlin or even in rival firms wouldn't be hard to do, and about Mefody's character, Kirill by then had become convinced: he was a freak through and through. But it was a false alarm; his younger brother seemed not to have even noticed his father's death. When he got back to Moscow, he signed over to his brother the power to control the business, and then kept on nibbling away at the family fortune as much as his little midget's appetite could handle. And Kirill, although he tried to emulate his father by remaining in the shadows, quickly turned into a celebrity throughout Rublyovka—there aren't so many young, handsome, unmarried billionaires in the world. Millions of girls and some lifestyle columnists stood by in the hopes that Kirill would decide to finally marry, but a year went by, and then a second, and then a third and fourth, and the bachelor's reputation became an important part of the head of Vremya corporation's image. All it took was for him to give another interview, answering the same old questions, saying something like, "Sex and humanism are not comrades" or "You don't bang your blood," and the rumors would start to circulate around Moscow with a redoubled intensity that Kirill Magomedov was gay or some sort of terrible pervert. Someone even said that he would hire prostitutes for some insane amount of money, drag them to his place, undress them, sit them on the grand piano (why a grand piano?), and with one hand would play Soviet songs while masturbating with the other.

Meanwhile, for some reason there weren't any rumors about Mefody, though he, of course, deserved them; but, obviously, the idea of a midget-billionaire was too much even for the most elite circles of Moscow. It's possible that even if some tabloid wrote that the co-owner of Vremya-Kapital was a midget, no one would believe such a tale. A pedophile, a drug addict, a fascist? Fine, no problem… but a midget—that's just absurd.

Mefody, it seemed, had gotten used to being such an absurdity long ago, this role fit him fine—so, at least, it seemed to Kirill, and also to Slava, a young retired FPS captain who served Mefody in the role of an aide, who had at one time served as the security to Patriarch Alexy, and was now responsible for Mefody's everyday comfort. They spent a lot of time in conversation together; Mefody loved to listen to stories about the patriarch's everyday life, especially about when the patriarch had died at his dacha in Peredelkino. Slava told the stories with pleasure, and then he would go report to Kirill in his office on the next-to-last floor of the *Federatsiya* tower; he told him honestly that everything was all right and that Mefody wasn't planning any kind of takeover or attempts on his brother's wealth.

Mefody, devil take him, really wasn't planning any kind of takeovers, he sincerely loved his brother, and regarding his troublesome personality—you'd act that way too if you had to live for even a few hours with such a deformity. Mefody tried not to think about what might happen to him the next day, or a week from now, or after a year, but when, flipping through the channels, he came upon Malakhov shouting something about some midget who had mysteriously grown, he immediately called Slava and ordered him to find this developed midget and bring him to Rublyovka right away.

While Vasya was being brought to Barvikha, Mefody ran around his study from one end to the other, and by the time Vasya showed up he had gotten really tired, so the sofa and the pose hadn't been planned; the fact is, he really couldn't stand on his own two feet from fatigue and, yes, from excitement as well. Yes, there was a ninety-percent chance that this whole story about the growth was a complete fabrication from beginning to end, but if there was even a microscopic chance that Vasya really had grown in the course of two weeks, then he, Mefody, would manage to shake the secrets out of Vasya and then use them to make himself grow. He had never really given it a thought, but this really was Mefody Arkadievich Magomedov's greatest dream.

Vasya, of course, wasn't about to spill Karpov's secret to the first person he met, but the first person he met started talking about money, and Vasya screwed up his face for a second, then exhaled: "Five thousand dollars." He felt scared; the sum seemed incredibly large. But Mefody silently got up from the sofa and without a word stepped up to his table on his little feet—tap-tap-tap—took an envelope out of the drawer:

"Here's ten," he said, waving it in Vasya's face. "Talk."

Vasya told him everything he knew: the man's last name was Karpov; he didn't know where he lived or where he worked; his cell-phone number was this and that; his address was such and such; one intravenous injection and a recommended diet; and he didn't take any money for the injection.

"May I go now?"

"Hey, take the money," Mefody handed him the envelope. Vasya noticed that his interlocutor smiled for the first time in the whole conversation—but very awkwardly, for some reason.

XI

IT ONLY TOOK SLAVA half a minute to find out Karpov's home address; he printed it out and brought Mefody the printout and stood at attention by the door, awaiting further orders. Mefody dismissed Slava with a wave to let him know he would call for him. It was obvious that he shouldn't call but go there himself—who knew how Karpov would react to a call out of the blue from a total stranger who knew what was going on in his mind. For obvious reasons Mefody had seen too many movies in his life, and all too easily called to mind images of demented mad scientists obsessed with ideas of taking over the world, and provincial loonies, tinkering with perpetual motion in their garage (Mefody had gone through a period of being entertained by Soviet movies at one point).

Within an hour Slava was driving Mefody to the third
terminal at Vnukovo Airport, and after three hours the
Falcon 7X with its lone passenger on board landed at a small
airport in the south of Russia; this was the first-ever business jet to land there in the history of the airport, and the
air traffic controllers had prepared a celebratory welcome
table for the occasion, complete with a locally-made cognac,
Praskoveya—over the next month, Mefody, who had never
heard of this cognac before, would drink so much of it that
at some point he would decide to buy a local cognac distillery
when he returned to Moscow. But that would happen later,
for now Mefody was being driven by Slava's colleague in the
FPS that he had contacted for the occasion—there's no better
guarantee for confidentiality than a personal relationship.
This guy (Mefody would never remember his name) had
also served as a patriarch's guard at one point, but then he
returned to his native region and started a transportation
business, and now, at Slava's request, was himself taking
Mefody to where he needed to go. We're not going to be
ironic about this guy's transportation business—it was not
so much transportation-related as it was ceremonial: in the
dark a Lexus hearse could pass for an official state vehicle
(all the more so since they really were a ceremonial class),

and Mefody, like all midgets, wasn't superstitious at all, and just laughed at how silly everything was the provinces.

The security keypad at the entrance was broken; Mefody stepped into the darkness, realized there was no elevator either, and angrily took the stairs. He rang for a long time at the door, which was finally opened by a sleepy Karpov, and while Mefody tried to come up with the right words to start the conversation, the master of the house himself, having invited the guest in, started to call for his wife, shouting, "Hey, it seems like the midget grapevine is working, and Vasya sent his friend over."

"He's not my friend," Mefody mumbled, and having let his receiving party extract some information about Vasya from him ("Yes, something like one meter sixty centimeters or more, excellent complexion, and happy."), he could finally move on to the heart of the matter. He knew that Karpov held some kind of secret that could transform short people into tall ones, and he wanted the same experiment performed on himself as had been done on Vasya. He was ready to pay or, if Karpov was interested, even to discuss the possibility of further business cooperation, in the long run, Mefody had the resources to turn an ingenious idea into a profitable business.

Karpov was confused. He had known that an investor would find him, but he didn't think that it would happen right here and now, when he couldn't even say with full certainty that his invention worked. Yes, he used the serum on Vasya, but to start processing it right then, no, it's too soon, but if Mefody will come back in three months or so, then the they could have a more substantial conversation, but for now—have some borscht, if you're hungry. If not, here's some coffee.

Certain that he was talking to a schizophrenic, Mefody, for his part, settled down—first, it's always easier when you know who you're dealing with; and second, schizophrenics are, as a rule, open to suggestion, and it shouldn't be too hard to talk Karpov into giving him an injection.

"So you want to get taller too?" Karpov suddenly realized and for some reason gave another happy laugh. "Listen, of course, it's no big deal. Let's just talk about compensation."

Mefody recalled how Vasya's face had screwed up when he asked for the five thousand, and as then smiled—it would be interesting to compare the requests of these two idiots, the one from the circus and this one. He asked, "How much?" and, you have to give credit to Karpov, was genuinely surprised when his interlocutor said that he wouldn't charge Mefody a kopeck, but he would ask him to spend two weeks—the amount of time needed to grow fully—here, in his apartment, because it was very important and necessary for Karpov to observe the process of growth in his test midget—it's a pity that it didn't work out with Vasya, but this time Karpov wasn't going to miss the opportunity.

It wasn't Mefody's intention to stay at the apartment; the hearse was waiting downstairs, and the Falcon at the airport—the billionaire hesitated for a second, and then thought that it might be even better this way. He sent Slava an explanatory text message and then answered that it would be a pleasure to stay with Karpov. And Karpov was already coming out of his room joyfully waving the syringe with the yellowish liquid.

XII

AND YOU DON'T NEED to think that Mefody was malicious, because he wasn't, but even if he was malicious, then it definitely wasn't directed at his own brother. He loved Kirill more than anybody in the world, and it wasn't Mefody's fault that he'd hardly ever made his brother happy for all these years. But now he was going to catch up; he had come up with a real surprise, a surprise to end all surprises. Well, of course, how had he not thought of it right away? His brother wouldn't see him the next day, but only after two weeks, and he wouldn't see a midget but a normal, grown-up man, who would be able to appear at the meeting of the board of directors, and at negotiations, and at *Pioneer* readings, without the slightest shame at his appearance, because his appearance would very soon be not just ordinary, but the most ordinary in the whole world—Mefody was imagining this so feverishly that he fell asleep only when the red sun of dawn appeared in the window. And he slept through the day until evening.

And in the evening Karpov, who smelled of something terrible, spent a long time measuring Mefody with a tape measure, then asked him about all kinds of things—beginning with childhood illnesses and leading to the average number of calories in Mefody's normal diet. Then the three of them—Mefody, Karpov and Marina—had eaten the leftover not-so-good borscht, then drank coffee, and it suddenly seemed to Mefody that these nice people were his own family, his real parents, and maybe he should think about turning his back on his on his family's billions and just staying with these people. Mefody had since childhood loved to imagine various horrors, so as to later enjoy the realization that he had only been a game in his imagination, and everything was really fine and just the same.

Then he really began to grow, and the expensive suit that he had been wearing when he arrived at Karpov's that night became too small for him, and Mefody agreed to give it away without regrets to Aunt Katya from next door whose grandson didn't have anything to wear to school. In return, the billionaire received a pair of sweatpants and a sweatshirt that had belonged to Katya's deceased husband, and he had the great pleasure of sitting in front of the mirror in those rags knowing that the next day they too would also be too small for him, and then he would have to borrow some jeans from the tall Karpov. Although he didn't have to borrow them, he could just go to a normal, ordinary store and buy himself some ordinary clothes without having to order them specially, in the strictest secrecy (the Italian tailors signed non-disclosure papers drawn up by Slava on FPS letterhead and translated into English and Italian). With every new centimeter added, life became more and more wonderful.

XIII

WHILE MEFODY GREW, Karpov, keeping Mefody as a potential investor in his mind, of course, followed his original plan, which meant storming the gates of heaven should begin with the most insignificant step. Though, in reality, however, there were even more necessary steps than Karpov could have foreseen, and he had already managed to curse himself repeatedly for the decision to walk and not just take a cab.

The town where Karpov settled with Marina was officially not even a real town, but rather a neighborhood district that was part of the small city. When Karpov would come here as a child there was no city yet, it was just a village, and city status was assigned to it the day after his grandfather's death; Karpov, who was then, as you would expect, a cynical teenager, joked that this had been done only to ensure that if his grandfather decided to return he would get lost—he would search for the village but there wouldn't be any village left. Now, fifteen years later, his own joke no longer seemed funny to him, but Karpov had still not come across any other explanations for the redesignation of the village into the city—a village it had been and a village it remained—and this was quite convenient for Karpov—the rural lifestyle of the local inhabitants was to provide him with important support. But he was able to quickly see that peasant ways of life have both pluses and minuses, and one of those minuses was before him right then in the form of a young, unsympathetic woman sitting at the desk for the classified section of the local paper, *Our Life* (in Karpov's childhood it had been called *Communist Beacon*). Blinking, she explained to him that if the service wasn't officially certified, then no one would place the classified, and if he didn't like it, then he needed come back after a month and complain to the editor, but for now the editor was on vacation, and as it is I've already talked with you for too long.

Having mentally characterized his interlocutor as a rural Soviet relic, Karpov asked her if she had a copy machine.

The rural Soviet relic didn't have a copy machine, but she showed Karpov how to get to the post office. At the post office he took a government-issue ballpoint pen and wrote out that if someone had a piglet, calf or lamb, then for five hundred rubles he'd like to borrow this animal; and then the piglet, calf or lamb could be exchanged for a large sheep, cow or pig as payment upon receipt a week later. He paused to think whether he should include his phone number, and then decided it wasn't worth it; he simply indicated the location of his shack and the time—tomorrow morning at nine o'clock—and, pleased with himself, made twenty copies, and at the same time bought a tube of glue and headed home, at every turn pasting his ad on poles and fences.

Surprisingly, the next morning Karpov encountered around eight local residents by the shack who looked as if they had been specially selected for a photo shoot of the "The Common Peoples of Rural Southern Russia." They included a timid, suntanned grandmother in a snow-white headscarf and a clearly intoxicated man in a dusty jacket and cap (he had most likely taken the calf without asking his wife, and a week later he would steal the money from her and sell the cow too) and a teenager with a fishing rod and a young goat (Karpov had not mentioned goats in his ad, he forgot)—basically, a feast for the eyes, but without any audience. Having recorded in his notebook to whom each animal belonged, Karpov gave each of his clients his cell number and told them to come back for their animals in a week's time. On the one hand, Karpov didn't feel any particular confidence from these people, but on the other hand they did come to him of their own volition, bringing their piglets and calves—so he didn't feel sorry if each of these visitors would spend the whole week in masochistic certainty that—clearly by the will of some evil external forces—they had become the victim of a cunning deception.

Having dismissed the visitors, Karpov began giving injections, cursing himself as a dilettante—surely there must be some sort of special veterinary syringes more useful than these one-off "users" that he had bought back in Moscow at the pharmacy chain 36'6. It was also good that Gennady was around; he at least knew something about agricultural practices, and without his help the test animals would have scattered.

Karpov and Gennady found places for the piglets in the barn, tied the young goat up outside the barn, and Gennady led the calves to the town park where there was an overgrown playground with a gated fence, and he even volunteered to keep watch over them until evening with a shepherd's vigilance. Gennady was already aware of the fact that Karpov was using his injections to grow these young animals into fully-grown adults, but he was so skeptical that he didn't dare say anything to anybody about them for fear they would just laugh at him. But the animals grew, and then a week later, checking his notebook, Karpov returned to their owners the pigs, cows, and the one goat, and then, standing in front of Gennady, in embarrassment counted out the money, yes, exactly four thousand (he handed a thousand to Gennady, who was offended, "Give me five hundred, what's this thousand about?!"). The military pensioner understood that he was witness to an amazing event that had the potential to radically change, among other things, his, Gennady's, life.

XIV

GENNADY PETROVICH FISHCHENKO, without asking for it, but not denying it either, turned into his own kind of sales manager—he chatted with clients, kept a schedule of the days and weeks ahead, and he even joked with them, saying, "There's no place in the queue until the end of next month, lady, but your calf will grow all by himself during this time, and you won't have to pay." Rumor of the magical serum spread with a rapidity that pleased Karpov: it was neither too frenzied nor too calm, and his worst nightmares—and yes, even Karpov had nightmares—of an endless space filled with so many animals that he wouldn't know where to put them all remained only nightmares. Now that some time had passed, you could probably say that Karpov had been, of course, simple-minded, because crowds of pigs and goats isn't a nightmare, but abundance; whereas a nightmare is when you are being talked about a kilometer from your shack and you don't know anything about it.

In the meantime, in a two-story, red-brick building exactly one kilometer from the shack at a table in a parlor by a fireplace (a yellow, strange-looking coquina fireplace), sat two men, red-faced, looking one much like the other. One of them had just arrived from the regional center, the general director of the Holy Rus' Meat-Processing Corporation, Valentin Vyacheslavovich Rusak, while the other, the red-brick building's owner, Nikolai Georgievich Filimonenko, *ataman* of the regional Cossack Council, was one of Rusak's five main meat suppliers. They had heard the news at the same time from different sources that some goon in the institute town was growing piglets into whole pigs in a week's time, and they both called the other at once—and got busy signals. Both Rusak and Filimonenko were alarmed by the news, and now they were trying to combine their forces to understand how this might affect their business.

Even if it turned out that the miracle would be limited territorially to only the town and the closest surrounding suburbs, the city market (they call it a "bazaar" around here) would be oversaturated with cheap meat within a month; and Valentin Vyacheslavovich considered that fine, because the cost of meat would cheapen, while the price of Holy Rus' kielbasa would not—no, therefore his expenses on raw materials would go down, but the profit would stay the same. Nikolai Georgievich agreed—yes, the meat at the bazaar would become cheaper, and he, of course, would lower the asking price for Valentin Vyacheslavovich, but we're both smart men here, and we understand that "if the miracle will be limited territorially," it won't work, and the best scenario would be that meat traders would come to the town for the meat, and most likely for the serum, not only from this region, but also from the Kuban, and from the Don, and from other places as far away as Chechnya. At the word "Chechnya," they fell silent, because they remembered well what had gone on here before the first campaign, when the bazaar and, generally, the whole local market was controlled by Chechens. That was awful, though it was brief.

"Maybe you should consult with the boys in Moscow?" Filimonenko asked hesitantly, and he was right to be hesitant; Rusak waved his hands: whoa, whoa, the moment they realize they don't need *our* meat, they'll come in here and take the serum for themselves, and within six months some Mikoyan would show up with kielbasa for two twenty, and that would be it, we wouldn't be able to do anything. Filimonenko nodded, reached up for a bottle of *Praskoveya* cognac on the shelf and poured some out; there sure were some things to think over.

XV

WHEN KARPOV CAME HOME and found only charred remains where his shack had once stood, he was, of course, surprised—but just surprised, nothing more. He didn't sit down in the ashes, holding his head in his hands, repeating, "Why, oh why?" Though, of course, it would be interesting to know who burned down the shack and why, but it wasn't as though he was about to sit in the ashes, clutching his head in his hands. He strolled around the ruins, and then went back to the house. He sat at the computer and was about to write on Twitter—"I hate them, these holy Russian peasants!"—but he thought better of it, went on checking his mail, and found out that he and Marina were no longer friends on Facebook.

One time, about five years ago, he and Marina got back from some kind of party, both slightly drunk or, even, perhaps, Marina was slightly drunk while Karpov was really drunk, and there had been a half-bottle of whiskey at home, and they decided to stay up a little longer; Marina drank a bit and then fell asleep, saying, "Sorry, that's it for me," while Karpov poured the rest of the whiskey into his glass, put the glass down on the computer table, and it suddenly dawned on him (drunks have this thing: they come up with something and it seems so amazing, "God, how cool and awesome is this!") that the blue glass with brownish liquid in it against the background of the white plastic of the computer was all so beautiful, and he, before drinking, took a picture of the glass, posted the photo to LiveJournal, then looked at his results—and it seemed like it really had come out so beautiful, but then, seeing his whiskey glass on the computer monitor, he somehow all of a sudden realized that he didn't need to finish the glass, he could let it stay to the morning, by this point Karpov was drunk enough to go to sleep peacefully, but the way he was going, he'd drink some more and start to puke and be ashamed of himself.

In the morning, of course, he poured the contents of the glass down the kitchen sink, but the story itself of the photograph on LiveJournal that had kept him from getting totally wasted made a lasting impression on Karpov; he often recalled this episode later, referring to himself as a member of the blog culture, and likely he was actually quite proud of it. And now, seeing that Marina had unfriended him on Facebook—well, it was only then, looking at it through the monitor, that Karpov finally realized it was over, that Marina had left him.

He hadn't heard her leave, he was sleeping, and when he woke up, he saw a note on the sheet next to him, in which Marina wrote that he was dear to her and generally "of the ultimate essence," but she couldn't live with him anymore because she had fallen in love with somebody else (when he read this he thought to himself, "Who is this somebody else, and could she have found that somebody else around here?") and now she was flying to Moscow with Mefody Magomedov, she was asking him not to miss her and, better yet, to forget about her completely and to find himself another good woman who would agree to share with him all of the joys of his discoveries, and that she didn't want to share them with him anymore because she deserved more, and it's not her fault that Karpov is too self-absorbed to give her that "more." She must have put a great effort into writing it. Karpov smiled; he really didn't believe that Marina could leave him and decided that if that's the way it had to be, then he could go back to sleep for another hour and a half.

Meanwhile at that very moment the merciless Falcon 7X was carrying Marina off to the north with her companion—a handsome brunette of medium height, in whom the former midget Mefody Arkadievich Magomedov would have been unrecognizable, even to his deceased mother (who had been killed in 1993 as a result of an assassination: an unknown assailant had thrown a hand grenade through the open window of her car; they buried her in a closed casket, and the killer has never been found). Mefody was wearing light-colored trousers and a t-shirt with "Lucky" printed on it; he and Marina had gone to the regional shopping center to buy some clothes the day before, and then, in a café on the main boulevard, he made his declaration—of course, Marina wasn't to blame for being the only woman around Mefody at the moment when he first felt himself to be a full-bodied man, but he really had fallen in love with her, and she herself, though she knew that it wasn't good to dump Karpov, and in fact she was still in love with him, she also understood that another chance like this wouldn't come her way again (when she thought about it, instead of the word "chance," she thought of the words "social elevator"; for some reason she, just like Karpov, switched on an inner official complete with bureaucratic terminology in moments of great excitement) and that Karpov, when he calmed down, would of course forgive her. At some point in the future, she would be driving by in a Jaguar and would extend a hand, and he'd understand that he'd never be a stranger to her.

So she had thought yesterday, but today she was met at the Vnukovo-3 airport by a morose man with light eyes in a nice suit—our old friend Slava—who, of course, kept the promise he had given Mefody two weeks ago not to tell a living soul where and why Mefody had flown away.

XVI

"GOING HOME?" Slava asked, trying not to act discomfited by Mefody's new appearance.

"I don't know," Mefody responded, suddenly at a loss, but he quickly got ahold of himself and asked to be taken, with Marina, to the Ritz-Carlton—there they could all talk together.

The conversation was short. Mefody again asked Slava not to say anything to Kirill and basically to behave as though Mefody was still traveling around somewhere far from Moscow. Slava promised that he wouldn't let him down and took the opportunity to compliment Mefody's companion: she's a beautiful girl and it's plain to see she's a good person too. Then he left, while Mefody and Marina stayed to spend the night in the hotel. They ate breakfast

with a view of the Kremlin, then Mefody sent Marina off to
Tretyakovsky Drive ("Find yourself some clothes") and took
himself for a walk a ways up Tverskaya (damn, for the first
time in his life he was actually walking on a street in the
center of Moscow!), and with a wave of the hand, flagged
a cab—also for the first time in his life.

Now everything amazed him: the nightmarish Humor
FM in the gypsy cab and the gypsy cab driver himself (who
was obviously a Tajik), and the traffic jam on the Third Ring,
and the skyscrapers of the Moscow-City business center—
still under construction—which Mefody was also seeing
for the first time in his life. This feeling that everything
that was happening to him right then—for the first time in
his life—made him feel crazy and, gasping in amazement,
Mefody made a great effort not to burst into tears, and suddenly understood that the emotion he felt wasn't joy. The
thing was that he was afraid, he'd never felt such a terror
before. At some point his teeth even started chattering.

The security at the entrance to the tower politely listened to what Mefody had to say and allowed him to call
up to Kirill's waiting room. Mefody dialed four twos, a
pleasant female voice answered: "Hello, Vremya-Kapital,"
and Mefody, feeling that his voice was shaking, informed

the receiver that he needed to see Kirill Arkadievich, to whom his unfortunate younger brother sends his regards, at once.

Mefody was expecting Kirill to be in a meeting or involved in some important negotiations, or simply to be holed up in his office, doing something important, asking not to be disturbed by any calls, but the hold music played no longer than a minute, and the secretary told Mefody to come up and that Kirill Arkadievich would receive him right away.

It's easy to understand Kirill's situation—everyone knew that he had a brother, but not everyone knew that fifteen days had already passed since he'd heard anything from his brother, who had conveyed a vague message through his assistant ("I've decided to head south")—usually Mefody called to check in when he was traveling, irritating his brother, and Kirill was himself surprised to find that Mefody's silence was no less irritating—who knew what trouble this dwarf could get into? Maybe he had been killed, maybe kidnapped, or maybe he found himself a lady-dwarf and was going to build her a seven-star hotel on the Mediterranean coast of Turkey—he had the means to do that. So when he heard that some guy had shown up

117

with a message from his brother, Kirill, of course, gave the order to bring the guy in to him at once.

And now a handsome brunette of medium height sat smiling in the guest chair in front of Kirill, enjoying the view of Moscow through the floor-to-ceiling office windows, not in any rush to explain what had happened to Mefody. Kirill told him that he had little time and that if the guest didn't want to talk to him, then perhaps he would like to have a word with his security service. Mefody snapped to and answered that Kirill shouldn't worry, his brother was all right, and moreover—he was already in Moscow. "In Barvikha?" Kirill asked, and Mefody answered, no, no, right here in Moscow, and in fact, in this very Federation Tower. Kirill reached for the phone; Mefody again felt afraid that his brother's nerves could ruin the surprise and, hating himself for his frightened voice, asked:

"You really don't recognize me?"

Kirill said nothing, but looked at his guest with curiosity. In his thirty-six years the billionaire had seen lots of things, and, as a matter of principle, an adult-size midget didn't seem to him like something that could absolutely ever happen. But really, who said that Mefody couldn't grow to adult size in two weeks?

Meanwhile, Mefody explained about Vasya, about the hearse at the airport, about Karpov, about the borscht, about Marina ("You'll be sure to like her"), about Slava, who had turned out to be a good fellow and hadn't told Kirill anything ("While we're at it, why not?" Kirill mentally asked Slava; for the primary duty of the retired captain was really to report everything that Mefody did). Kirill listened and said nothing, and when Mefody stopped talking—and he had already said everything he had to say—the silence became uncomfortable, and Mefody was the first to give in and cried out to his brother: "Kiri-i-i-iill!"

Kirill, returning to his senses, looked intently at the man sitting before him and asked very gravely:

"I have only one question for you. What have you done with my brother Mefody? What. Have. You. Done. With him."

XVII

KIRILL REALLY HAD UNDERSTOOD everything right away—well, not exactly right away, but when Mefody asked if his brother recognized him, Kirill nearly nodded—he did. And so he didn't listen very intently to his story—it didn't matter in the end who the douchebag was who had injected some shit into Mefody's vein. While Mefody was talking, Kirill looked at him and as he gradually calmed down noticed with satisfaction that it was nearly impossible to find facial features in this man that were similar to those of the Mefody he knew. When Mefody finished his tale, Kirill had already devised the appropriate facial expression and tone of voice. It was the same tone with which Putin had once spoken to him.

"I have only one question for you. What have you done with my brother Mefody? What have you done with him?"

And walking to the window, he turned away, awaiting a response. If Mefody had looked closer at the reflection of Kirill's face in the window, he would have seen that his brother was smiling. But Mefody didn't look any closer, he still thought that this was some kind of game—his game, his surprise.

"Ha ha ha," he tried to laugh. "You really didn't recognize me!" He jumped out of the guest chair, came up to his brother (who didn't turn around) and tried to put his arms around his shoulders. His brother stepped aside. Now Mefody stood by the window alone, and Kirill thought that it would be great if this person, at this moment, would break the window and throw his customized body out, freeing Kirill from the necessity of having to continue with this ridiculous scene.

"Listen," Mefody said again in a frightened tone. "If you don't believe me, let's call Slava, he knows the story."

"And who told you about Slava?" Kirill answered in a bored voice, but he went ahead and pushed a button and asked the secretary to find Mefody's assistant and call him into the office. Slava was in Barvikha, the ride took forty minutes—in the meantime, Kirill relocated Mefody out of the office, but not into the waiting room, but into a conference room, and closed the door so Mefody didn't see how Slava entering Kirill's office. When Mefody next saw Kirill, he was together with Slava.

"Well," Kirill joyously asked. "Look familiar?"

"Yeah, not really," Slava answered, and Mefody realized there had been a change.

Kirill again put on his worried expression and, addressing himself primarily to Mefody, informed Slava that the crappiest thing in this whole situation was that it was not at all clear where his unfortunate brother had disappeared to, but seeing as how this guy—a nod in Mefody's direction—had just seriously tried to pretend that he was *him*—obviously he knew something, and Kirill was placing his hopes on Slava, for his professionalism and experience, and was tasking him to work with this scumbag to find out the real story.

"Slava," Mefody said, now really terrified, "we aren't joking around any more, tell him everything."

"Now *you* will tell *me* everything," Slava answered gravely and, letting Kirill out of the room, strode over to Mefody. "Shall we talk?"

XVIII

"HE KNOWS NOTHING," Slava shrugged an hour later in Kirill's office. "He seems crazy. I took him to the Metro and came right back."

"Thank you," Kirill shook his hand. "I hope you understand that I know..." Kirill suddenly paused. "I know how to say 'thank you.'"

Slava understood. He was proud of himself—he hadn't broken, hadn't given himself away, not even when left alone with Mefody; and Mefody, even when he understood that Slava was no ally, plaintively repeated, "Remember, remember!" Slava remembered everything, but what he remembered no longer had anything to do with the adult-size Mefody. Giving Mefody a shakedown, he took away his passport and his wallet, but honestly—Slava isn't some kind of brute—returned all the cash to its owner, fifteen and something thousand rubles. Then he escorted Mefody down in the elevator, put him in the car, and drove him to the Metro. In parting, he asked him not to show his face again, although he knew that Mefody would come back.

He did come back—that same night—to the restaurant Color of the Night, where Kirill was giving a lecture on the theme of "The Tao of Winnie the Pooh"; the cover was a thousand rubles, and Mefody paid for a ticket just to go over to his brother and once again see him recoil and shout to his security to take this psycho away. The private security guards who worked at Color of the Night weren't of the experienced variety. They didn't know how to beat someone up properly, without leaving marks on the body; and Mefody saw Slava—from upside down while lying on the floor—through a veil of blood dripping down his face. Slava extended a hand: "Get up, let's go," and dragged the sobbing Mefody to the toilet, led him to the sink, where he let him wash the blood from his face, and then taking his face in his hands, forced Mefody's jaws apart, placed a pill under his tongue and, keeping hold of his elbow, waited as Mefody slowly sank to the tile floor. He bent down, checked his pulse—there was no pulse—came out of the toilet, went up to security, and, pointing to the open door, guiltily pronounced, "A heart attack, looks like."

While Mefody was being beaten, he thought that Marina would likely get upset when she saw his smashed face, and she might even cry when he told her about the day's adventures. But even if he had stayed alive and gone back to the hotel, instead of Marina he would have found a note in the room that said that she realized that she made a mistake, that she had been wrong to leave Karpov and was now returning to him, and for Mefody to not come looking for her.

She wrote the note fifteen minutes after parting from Mefody on Tverskaya—she descended into the underground crosswalk, came out on the other side, then stopped and quickly went back.

Then she walked out of the hotel onto the street, descended into the Metro, bought a twenty-ride ticket, and headed to her mom's place at Taganka.

XIX

IN THIS TIME, Karpov tried not to think about Marina, not in the "forget-about-that-whore" sense but—well, why upset yourself more when it's out of your control, especially if there are circumstances that require immediate intervention—his shack—for the demise of which you needed to hand it to Karpov—he didn't for a second try to link it to the disappearance of Marina and Mefody, he reasoned that even though the oligarch midget was a scoundrel, he had no reason to burn down Karpov's shack; even if he supposed that Mefody had taken offense at something, it would have been sufficient revenge on Karpov just to run off with his wife. So regarding the shack, Karpov came up with two, well, to be exact, one and a half possible scenarios. The first: local hoodlums, some punks, or *gopniki*—"We saw the night, walked all night till morning"—they see that a shack, they think, hey, let's burn it down. This is the first scenario, the less interesting one.

The second was profoundly conspiratorial in nature, and so Karpov treated it like half of a version; he didn't believe in conspiracies. He didn't want to be friends with Elena Nikolaevna? He didn't. And she was, by the way, in charge here, in a good way (not in a good way, of course, but quite the opposite, in a bad way, but it doesn't matter in this case), and she might very well have used this vandalistic method to convey the message to Karpov that on her territory he's an unwanted person and that if he still wanted to cultivate calves and piglets, then let him choose some other place for his experiments.

The question, "Who is to blame?", it must be said, had quite an optional significance—even if he was able to figure out who had burned down the shack, he wouldn't do anything to the offender; he would just be upset. Much more interesting was the question of what is to be done. Karpov loved to say (these were really Marina's words, but Karpov was in agreement with her) that a real man must always have a plan. And Karpov also had an important addition to this formula: yes, a plan is always needed, but what makes a plan a good one is that you can always modify it, "Let's replace the scene at the stadium with a scene in a telephone booth"; so now, pacing back and forth in the long corridor of his grandfather's apartment, Karpov pondered ways of modifying his original plan. He thought and thought—and then he got it.

XX

AN OLD WATCHMAN was on duty at the entrance to the institute—Karpov knew him from sight, they had run into each other somewhere in town, but he didn't know his name; and, having given the old man's hand a squeeze—here, ultimately, everyone was related somehow—he casually asked, jutting his chin upward:

"Is she in her office?"

"Nah," the old man answered. "She has visitors."

"Shall I wait?" But the old man, waving his hand to the side, said that it might be a long wait, that the director was actually showing the visitors around the exhibition hall, and that Karpov could go straight there—he, at any rate, didn't mind the old man.

The exhibition hall was a cramped room that was arranged something like a Soviet-era military propaganda room. The display stands, portraits, graphs and sheaves of some types of grain likely indicated accomplishments from the institute's past. Past the display stands and sheaves of grain, accompanied by a retinue made up of a dozen people, Elena Nikolaevna floated arm-in-arm with a short, thickset man, as wide as he was tall, who resembled a bulldog, whom Karpov recognized as the presidential envoy in this federal region. Another man might have turned around and left, but Karpov was not afraid of bureaucrats, and it seemed to him that moment might just turn out to be the right time for the conversation that he had thought up earlier that day. Nodding at the director (she apparently didn't recognize him—that is, of course she did, but she didn't let on, and Karpov considered such a reaction to be indirect evidence linking Elena Nikolaevna to the burning of the barn), he joined the tail of the retinue and began to listen to what the hostess was talking about with her guest.

The conversation (to be more precise, Elena Nikolaevna's monologue, as the envoy only nodded) revolved around the newest advancements in agricultural science.

"This," Elena Nikolaevna said, "is our pride and joy, branched wheat. There is one stalk, you see, but five or six ears; it's very economical."

The envoy nodded.

"And this," she said, gesturing in the direction of tables painstakingly detailed with magic markers showing two glued-on, Xeroxed pictures of some kinds of birds—a diagram that illustrated how with the right diet a jay can turn into a cuckoo. "Now don't be surprised, I wouldn't believe it myself if not for the work of our scientists. It's all very simple. We are what we eat. A cuckoo eats these, you know, furry worms. A jay doesn't eat them, but if we force it to—*voila*!" Elena Nikolaevna's finger traced an arc in the air and touched the bird on the right.

"That's funny," the envoy said, speaking for the first time. "But what does this mean to us from a practical point of view?"

"The principle is what is important!" Elena Nikolaevna started to ramble. "What's important is that if we want to get a specific result, we must want to get this result. A cuckoo and a jay—yes, this is a meaningful experiment whose application is most relevant for grains. One can produce rye using wheat, and moreover different types of rye can be produced using different types of wheat, and with those types of wheat you can produce oats, and oats can beget wild oats."

The envoy nodded.

"And this," Elena Nikolaevna said, pointing at a bottle with something black in it, "is a petroleum-based growth agent, PGA: a unique nutritional supplement, especially if you don't forget about our main source of wealth, oil, one that can produce fantastic results in livestock production."

Karpov thought that it was a shame that his granddad hadn't lived to see this, but the envoy, most likely, didn't think anything at all, because glancing somewhere past Elena Nikolaevna, he said:

"Everything is great, but I'll tell you frankly—I don't see any innovations here. Import substitution... yes, from the perspective of import substitution you deserve the highest praise; but you see, at one point we too excelled at import substitution. Maybe we were even too excellent at it. But, alas, I just don't see any innovations." It was then that Karpov realized that his time had come.

"Excuse me." Parting the crowd, he walked up to the bottle of his grandfather's PGA. The envoy, the director and their entourage all stared at Karpov, and Karpov eagerly started to explain that this was a nice exhibit and, of course, interesting enough, but not complete, and that its most important accomplishment was, unfortunately, lacking, but that he'd tell them all about it, if they didn't mind. Not giving time for them to answer, Karpov told them all about the rats and the piglets and the calves, remaining silent only about the midgets. The growth cycle lasted seven days, he had documented proof. Russia would become well-fed. The four *I*'s (Innovations, Investments, Institutes, Infrastructure) would be covered, with another two to boot: Ivan Ilyin (Karpov had read the papers and knew that the envoy had a weakness for the fascist-philosopher's works).

"Ivan Ilyin, is this the name of your serum?" The envoy perked up and now addressed Elena Nikolaevna: "You have introduced me to your colleague, but I seem to have forgotten his name."

"This is Doctor Karpov, our pride," Elena Nikolaevna Gorskaya exhaled. After half an hour, a letter to the Economic Ministry with a positive endorsement penned by the envoy was on her table, and at the table before a cup of coffee and a plate of stale Danish cookies sat the institute's newest senior research associate, Karpov.

XXI

NIKOLAI GEORGIEVICH FILIMONENKO, the ataman and meat distributor, of course, didn't believe what he saw on TV news, and he was suspicious that things weren't as spotless with the Sochi Olympics as Vladimir Posner said in all the ads. But that he—a modest and low-profile person, in general—was what the country needed to save the Olympics seemed to him like something out of the French comedy films that he had watched in his childhood, not anything real. He was weighing a bluish business card in his palm in a stunned silence. The business card read Olympstroi Corporation. OZERKOV, Vladislav Aleksandrovich. Managing Director.

"I am a business-minded person." Nikolai Georgievich always managed to choose the right tone in each conversation as they took place, and if the person he was talking to had interrupted him, then Filimonenko would have changed it right away. But his companion was silent.

"I am a business-minded person," the ataman repeated, "and I don't like superfluous introductions. If the Olympians need meat, they'll get meat, there's just one question: how much is needed and how much money do we have. You don't have to worry about the rest, Filimonenko has never failed anyone before."

His companion was silent, looking the ataman in the eye. Then he quietly said:

"When you guys burned down that asshole's shack, was the liquid in there?"

Nikolai Georgievich generally knew how to choose the right tone in a conversation, but now he lost his bearings. He looked at Vladislav Aleksandrovich as though for the first time—yeah, he looks KGB, but what does that mean? It could really mean anything, but Filimonenko correctly guessed that, sure enough, before him sat a former functionary of the Federal Services, but not from National Security, rather from Federal Protection; and he is already familiar to us, because while Mefody Magomedov was alive, Slava worked as his assistant.

And when Mefody had been cremated without so much as an autopsy, Slava brought the urn straight to Kirill's office in a big red sports bag with a white Cheburashka on it.

Kirill squeamishly pointed to the corner—put it over there, and as if he was continuing a just-interrupted conversation, said:

"Yes, I know how to say 'Thank you.' Your position, as you can guess, no longer exists. But this only means growth for your career. Olympstroi, are you familiar with this name?"

Slava was indeed.

XXII

TWO YEARS HAD PASSED since the president of the International Olympic Committee, Jacques Rogge, closing the organization's regular session—which was held in Guatemala—exhaled, "Sochi!" which unleashed a storm of excitement and happiness across the vast Russian expanses from Vladivostok to Kaliningrad. Two years passed and the happiness hadn't faded away, it only changed in its form—it no longer rumbled from sea to sea, but peacefully shone in the form of a small bronze plaque outside an expensive office a fifteen-minute walk from the Kremlin. Olympstroi was the most mysterious state-owned corporation in the country. Of course, its name was familiar to everyone—the newspapers regularly wrote about some construction blunders or about how the corporation had again changed its CEO—but in the grand scheme of things all of this news didn't have anything to do with its most important secret, and the corporation itself had even less to do with the upcoming Olympics than might appear to be the case. The person closest to the root of this mystery than anyone, but without actually realizing it, was the editor of the "Economics and Politics" section of *Kommersant*. For no particular reason, he put together a chart of who had come to work at Olympstroi and from where within the last year and a half and published it on his LiveJournal page. From that, it turned out that this wasn't any kind of corporation, but a sort of vacuum for professionals—even a quick glance at the chart revealed that for some mysterious reasons even the lowest positions at Olympstroi (up to the position of deputy departmental director) were filled by people who had eagerly relinquished their positions as ministers and governors and top-level managers of both state-owned and formally-privately-owned companies. Perhaps the creator of the chart could have guessed what the response would be, but by some maddening coincidence on exactly the same day that the chart with these names and positions appeared on his LiveJournal, some Internet asshole hacked the journalist's email account—thank God, he didn't touch his personal or work correspondence, limiting himself (possibly his signature trait to show off to other hackers) to stealing his LiveJournal password and erasing all of his posts over the past year. To mark his work the hacker left a picture of a popular Internet meme: Mikhail Boyarsky in a feathered hat with the slogan, "You are all faggots!" After two days, LiveJournal administrators deleted the hacked blog. The journalist was not upset, he had always treated LiveJournal as something fun but not too important. Incidentally, just after the chart was posted, the security service of Olympstroi was ordered to block every possible leak of new personnel decisions within the corporation. Because the most interesting thing to know about Olympstroi is that the construction of the Olympic facilities themselves was, let's put this carefully, a secondary component of the corporation's activities. Generally speaking, no one seriously expected that the Olympics in Sochi would take place—and Jacques Rogge was informed of this within a month following the ceremony in Guatemala—well, as it happens, Russia did not calculate its capabilities and resources properly, and the IOC had made a mistake, but on the bright side, there was enough time before the Olympics to find a reason to move them to Korea, which in contrast to our country, could be "understood with the mind," and which had been prepared for the Olympics long before their formal request to the IOC.

But Olympstroi had another, perhaps much more important, function than building stadiums and hotels. Using their unlimited capabilities, the corporation had been scrupulously monitoring and tracking any and all inventions and discoveries that had been achieved on Russian territory with interesting potential applications over the last three years. And if one were given a task, such as to gather one hundred of the most mysterious deaths and suicides that had taken place in the country over this time period, it would become immediately apparent that a large part of them were connected in one way or another with what went on behind the closed doors of the corporation. A manufacturing engineer in the Kaluga brewing factory, Nikita M., drowned in a vat of beer, an unfortunate accident that is intriguing enough as it is. But who knew that the deceased had his own original formulas for increasing the efficiency of beer production ten times over, which could allow his company break into the ranks of the leaders of the Russian brewing industry in a fantastically short period of time. So said the Olympstroi specialist, at any rate, waving some papers around when the leaders of all of the biggest brewing companies of the country had gathered in the company's head office to formally to discuss the new "Olympic" brand of beer and the opening up of bids for its production. They understood everything about the sensational technology immediately and accurately, and those voluntary donations "for the Olympics" that the beer industry was still sending into the budget of Olympstroi, possibly, could be considered the price of keeping the murdered Kaluga manufacturing engineer's idea from ever being realized.

But Slava had heard about the story about the beer from others—this happened before his time. His time began with the meat. The same kind of meeting, but now under his, Slava's, chairmanship—and the presenter was a fidgety red-faced fatass from somewhere in the south.

"Valentin Vyacheslavovich Rusak," Slava introduced the fatass, checking the name on his papers. Those gathered— the people who controlled the country's entire meat industry (all of it, up to and including kangaroo) were listening. They listened with horror, though what scared them was not so much the lone rider with his magic serum that the presenter was talking about, as the fees that Olympstroi, in the form of Slava, could request to prevent the magic serum from destroying the existing market balance for which many of those who sat before Slava at that moment had paid for with the blood of their partners, rivals, or whomever else. And not only with blood.

Therefore they were all quite surprised when Slava referred to money in a seemingly conciliatory tone—and he immediately realized that the usual charge for *not* using the invention in this situation was not the most important thing. He was most interested in the part of Rusak's report about how one of the overactive local meat distributors ("Fi-li-mo-nenko," Slava pronounced in his head, trying to remember the name) had either simply burned down the lone rider's laboratory or—and he didn't even want to think about it—had also destroyed the invention that could be useful both for the Olympic organization and also his own slush fund.

XXIII

"WHEN YOUR GUYS burned down that asshole's shack, was the liquid in there?" Slava repeated his question, and Filimonenko suddenly thought that he probably should have gone to the bathroom before his buzzer was rung—but you can't think of everything.

"I can't remember," he whined. "But I can check. I will definitely find out," he rephrased it, looking at Slava no longer pathetically, but with deep devotion—Nikolai Georgievich really could change his tune to match his companion's, as though he may be an ataman.

"You have twenty-four hours," Slava answered; he stood up and walked out without saying goodbye. That happened in the evening, but the next morning Slava called and said that his department had lost interest in the liquid and that if Filimonenko for some reason would like to talk to Karpov, then he could go right ahead; it no longer had anything to do with Slava. Slava could send shivers down the spine of his listeners just by the tone of his voice, but at that moment if he was mad at anyone, it was at himself; although perhaps he wasn't to blame, logistics are always tough in big schemes, and at least it's better that he received a call that day instead of a week later from someone at an unknown number who said that everything was fine with the serum, that the samples and the formula were already in Moscow. He headed to the airport, reasoning to himself that although his first mission had failed, in any case the second would soon follow, and that with this one there would be no misfire; some time back the deceased Patriarch had called Slava a quick learner and that meant something. With such thoughts, Slava took off over the hills crisscrossed by forest belts and fields; and somewhere below, on the third floor of a shabby Stalin-era building in the institute's town, Karpov was lying in a corridor on linoleum that had been set by his grandfather and trying to show with gestures that he was ready to talk, but with his Adam's apple pressed by a paratrooper's boot, the words got stuck in his throat. Filimonenko didn't understand him at first, but then he got it and said: "Take your foot off him," and the young Cossack captain with three St. George's crosses on his camouflage peasant's coat (Kolya Chernikov had really served in the Airborne Corps until the previous autumn, but the crosses had been presented to him by Filimonenko as a sort of advance honors), spit on Karpov between his eyes, dragged his boot off of Karpov's neck, and then Karpov could see Kolya's zipper—and it seemed that Kolya had an erection.

"Can I get up now?" Karpov lay where he was, realizing that he couldn't do anything without permission in this situation.

"Yeah, get up," Filimonenko apathetically answered, and Karpov hoisted himself up off the linoleum and stood at the same height as the ataman.

"So it was you who burned down my shed?" Without getting an answer, Karpov spit a piece of tooth onto the floor; he had been beaten up before, but this was the first time it had cost him a tooth, and, as a silly habit of his, he decided to make note of the date, but it turned out that he didn't know what day it was.

"This isn't right," he said to the ataman, who maintained his silence. "I also understand words, as a matter of fact."

And then he also fell silent, felt sorry for himself, and nearly shed tears.

XXIV

THE MAIN PURPOSE of Filimonenko's visit to Karpov was simply to brighten his mood, which had been ruined by Slava and his visit the evening prior. Filimonenko didn't like being made to feel afraid, especially when the source of the fear was just two or three or however many words Slava had used that evening. But while Kolya and his two partners were beating Karpov, Filimonenko first of all didn't feel any sense of satisfaction, because as a matter of fact, even if this chump was to blame, then it was only for his own stupidity; since no one had warned him about anything, he couldn't have expected it, and in his place Filimonenko wouldn't have expected anything either. Yes—in his place, precisely, and this was the second thing—the ataman suddenly thought that it might not be a bad idea to have a liter or two of this liquid. And when Karpov said that he could understand words as well, Filimonenko asked Kolya to "Fuck him up some more"—and Karpov collapsed, but the ataman said: "Well, it's been a pleasure, thanks, boys," and dismissed his guys, who left him alone with Karpov. Fifteen minutes later he walked out to his GMC with a newspaper-wrapped parcel from which protruded the neck of a two-liter Coca-Cola bottle filled with a yellowish liquid. If anyone had seen it, they would have thought that it was homebrew.

And a week later a discussion thread called "A Tiger" popped up on the town's Internet forum; naturally, some teenager had spotted a tiger in the fields behind the institute, and didn't just see it, but had been forced to flee through the forest belts, and he himself didn't know how he managed to outrun it. The only one who believed him was a Muscovite who suggested that perhaps the tiger had escaped from the zoo, but, of course, there were no zoos in the town, not even in the regional center, and posters quickly explained this to the Muscovite, but they didn't feel any need to explain anything to the teenager who started the thread, the rest of the replies to his post amounted to the forum's resident posters commenting they wouldn't be against meeting the dealer who had supplied such powerful weed to the guy who had come up with this tiger story. And when someone wrote, "Yes, I also saw something, but it wasn't a tiger, a tiger's hide has orange stripes, but this one was a kind of gray, sort of faded-looking, but on the other hand, anything will fade under the sun in these latitudes." Anyway, when this post appeared in the thread, everyone of course assumed that the author was the same as the first guy, or was just some other jokester, even though his joke wasn't that funny: a faded tiger, L-O-L.

But then the District Office of Civil Defense and Emergency Management issued a press release calling on citizens to remain calm, because there had been multiple sightings of a large predator from the cat family in the town's vicinity—they thought it to be a type of jungle cat or a lynx, but it had not yet been caught. Whoever saw the animal was advised to immediately call 01, or 112 if from a cell phone. After this bulletin, a trio of imposters immediately appeared on the forum, claiming that they had been the ones who wrote the first post about the tiger, but then someone wrote something about boobs and the discussion, as often happens on the Internet, came to a dead end.

Meanwhile the ataman Filimonenko was drinking—not because he regretted taking the bottle of serum from the unfortunate Karpov, but because things didn't turn out so well with the kitten, and he really should have started with piglets, but little pigs didn't interest the ataman, and the kitten was so cute, the ataman had even thought up a funny name for him—Galustyan. He carried him by the scruff of his neck, laid him out in the palm of his hand, and injected the entire syringe into his belly. The kitten yowled at first, and then drank a liter of milk within an hour. The ataman poured out some more—milk for Galustyan, vodka for himself—and rejoiced in how cool it was that there were kittens in the world.

But after four days Galustyan—already a burly cat that came up the ataman's waist—jumped over the fence and ran off somewhere. The ataman thought, "I should go find him," but then spit and occupied himself with other matters.

XXV

KARPOV DIDN'T UNDERSTAND what had happened at
the institute—on the one hand, the Federal Target Program,
"A Well-Fed Russia," had spelled out in black and white that
this institute should receive nine hundred million rubles
through 2020 for the development of innovative technologies in the cultivation of leguminous crops and livestock;
but on the other hand—all of the work on the serum,
which was now called "Ivan Ilyin"—dumb, of course, but
the envoy liked it—was suspended, and Elena Nikolaevna
herself could not explain what had happened. She didn't
really want to fire Karpov but, looking him not so much in
the eye as at his broken nose, told him that she wasn't sorry
about it and that she would be in his debt until the end of
her days, but he would hardly be interested in a position at

the institute at a salary of three thousand rubles; and the federal billion was, of course, a billion, but, first, she still hadn't figured out how she would cash it out, and secondly, she wasn't sure if would be fair to share the money with Karpov. Karpov didn't want to haggle, he had come to say goodbye anyway; he pulled a bottle of cognac out of his bag, and toward midnight, when Elena Nikolaevna had fallen asleep on his no-longer marital bed, Karpov, trying to move as stealthily as possible, got out from under her heavy forearm, went over to the computer, and wrote on Twitter: "I hatte scumbags"—with a typo, he was drunk, after all.

Then he finished off the vodka and fell asleep on the couch in the other room. When he woke up, Elena Nikolaevna was gone; he went into the kitchen, drank some water out of the tap, and looked out of the window—there was Gennady strolling along below. Karpov wanted to call out to Gennady from the window and invite him in, "I'm leaving, and I wanted to say goodbye," but then the doorbell rang—could it be Marina?—and, limping, he walked over to open the door. He didn't ask "Who's there?" although that wouldn't change anything anyway—an unknown man was standing in the foyer and waved an ID card and with the intonation of a standup comedian greeted him:

"Federal Security Bureau."

There were two of them. The one who had rung walked in while the second stayed outside on the stairs, but they could have both waited outside—all they required was for Karpov to get dressed and follow them outside. Outside, a white Niva SUV was waiting.

"It's mine, not the bureau's," sighed the one who had rung. Karpov was shoved in the back seat, and they drove off. Gennady silently stood and watched them as they left.

XXVI

I WANTED TO GO ON and write further about how the clock outside the window struck noon and the man in the office, having turned his attention from his papers, looked out the window and looked not at the clock but at the red star with golden streaks that crowned the clock tower and smiled, flaring his nostrils. But if I wrote that, the story would become unacceptable, because I have no idea what went on in that office or if its owner really did smile—and, excuse me, but I wouldn't like to make anything up, so I had better just skip ahead a few weeks.

Karpov, if you're interested, spent all these weeks locked in an apartment on Dzerzhinsky Street a minute's walk from the hotel that the Syrians had built when Karpov was a kid. No one asked him anything, no one talked to him at all, once every two days a woman would come and silently hand him a bag of food—sausages, *pelmeny*, bread—and then leave; and the rest of the time Karpov was left to himself. No phone, much less a computer, in the apartment; the books on the shelves were uninteresting—*Choose Your Enemy*, *Hour of the Owl*, *I've Been Ordered to Kill You*, and so on—and the television wasn't much good, and the only thing that Karpov might have been entertained by was Russian Radio, which, if listened to long enough, could plaster an idiotic smile on the face of even the unhappiest man.

So much for Karpov. His wife Marina, of course, was expecting his call; but she had continued to live at her mom's, not wanting to call Karpov yet, and she was right, because if she heard that his mobile number was not in service and no one was answering their home number, she would have gotten worried, and worrying generates cellulite, as the writer Alexander Terekhov would say. In other words, there was nothing interesting going on with Marina either; in general, if anything interesting was going on with anyone, it was only with the ataman Filimonenko, who, from any point of view, was "not so pleasant"—his comrades in the Cossack circle and the meat business had buried him in a closed coffin, trying not to look at each other, because no one had died such a horrible death in this region since the Civil War (when Foma Shpak, the famous *kombedovets*, had been sawed in half with a double-handled saw by anarchists). According to the version of the story spread on the Internet by the secret services, the ataman had been sliced up by some Caucasians who also, among other things, cut out his heart, possibly for some ritual purposes. The ataman's death led to a big gathering of people on Krepostnaya (formerly known as Komsomolskaya) Hill in the regional center, and people were even ready to take revenge on the Caucasians in the next marketplace over, but proper respect should be given to the leader of the local "Slavic Union," who kept the promise that he had personally given to the head of the regional police the day before, and appealed to the citizens to keep calm, "because Ramzan is standing at the entrance to the city, only waiting for us to make the first move so they can cut us up like pigs." The people, of course, were upset that they couldn't go to the marketplace, but Ramzan is an argument you can't do anything about.

There is no point in blaming the FSB and the cops for spreading the rumors about the circumstances surrounding Filimonenko's death; they manipulated the nationalistic sentiments in the region, there was no other way, because if people were to find out what really happened, nobody would believe any of it. It would be enough to say that even the local police officer who shot Galustyan when he, having disemboweled the ataman (cats who run away, as a rule, always come back home), and swallowed his heart, liver, and lungs, and had started in on Nikolai Georgievich's right leg—even the cop who shot Galustyan (his last name was very police-esque—Evsyukov) was recovering now in a regional psycho-neurological hospital—he lost his mind immediately after the predator died; doctors found him kissing the dead Galustyan on the nose, and even now they still cannot vouch for the officer's mental state.

But, as has been said before, this has nothing to do with the further course of events, because the plot of this story, having flown from the south to the north, made a few circles over Moscow, in particular up and around the Kremlin, moved northwest from the Russian capital and settled in the nice assisted living facility Soyuz, which had built by some federal corporation (not Olympstroi, in case you were wondering) in a former pioneer camp near the Novorizhskoe Highway that had been formally closed under quarantine for the swine flu by personal order of the Russian general health officer, Gennady Onishchenko.

XXVII

TALKING ABOUT THIS GUY makes me feel kind of uncomfortable—it's always awkward to talk about something that
no one would ever believe to be true, and I, in principle,
could avoid this awkwardness by calling my hero by his real
name but, first off, he's already sued journalists and bloggers
who unveiled his identity, and second, even his friends are
used to calling him by his LiveJournal nickname, which is
Close to Zero, therefore, you could go ahead and not believe
me, but what can you do, even I'm used to it.

It's funny, but Close to Zero was once even acquainted
with Karpov, LiveJournal is generally conducive to creat-
ing the most exotic circles of acquaintances; but they had
a fight long ago about some political crap, and not only did
they stop communicating, but also from time to time, not

calling each other by name of course, they would exchange painful personal attacks against each other on LiveJournal. In general, it seems to me that Karpov is a bit less to blame in this conflict, but I'm also ready to agree that in any conflict both sides are equally guilty, therefore, I confess, I just don't like Close to Zero, but I'll try to control myself in describing him.

Although a graduate of the Department of Sociology at Moscow State University with roots in Kemerovo, he was born in Mongolia; his parents worked in the Federal Trade Agency. He started to work in the '90s, I believe in '98 as a layout designer for a classifieds tabloid, then he worked in some elections, ended up in the Foundation for Effective Politics, worked there in various positions for six years or so, then he was let go—technically because of his weakness for participating in a historical re-enactors' movement, combined (for some reason among the fans of war games this was fairly common) with the filming of gay porn—but in fact, the official wording was for "amoral polemicizing methods"; still, he remained in political circles, he now belonged to the semiofficial circle of "realists," a.k.a.: "amoral reactionaries," whatever that meant, and as for how he earns a living, I heard from the guys at the bookstore

Falanster about him writing some reviews on non-fiction that are published once a week on some infrequently visited websites. That's Close to Zero for you.

And now he was riding in a truck that he had flagged down with a raised hand (he called this "doing a Roman salute") on the Novaya Riga Highway, watching road signs, and when the number on the kilometer marker matched what he had been told in Moscow, he got out of the truck and lit up a cigarette on the side of the road. He had no doubt that this was the start of a new life.

XXVIII

THE SECURITY GUARD at the assisted living facility's checkpoint, obviously not a local but someone who had been sent by the same program that had arrived with the document from Onishchenko regarding the quarantine, spent a long time inspecting the guest's passport, then put it in the scanner, and even for some reason pressed the scanner's cover down with his hand; Close to Zero could see the raw skin on the knuckles of the security guard's hand. Then the security guard called someone, and within a minute Close to Zero was already shaking hands with a smiling man in a jacket without a tie—he looked like either a program director or just a man with a high degree of self-esteem.

"First, I want to understand how much they told you about what we need from you," the director began as they walked along a cobblestone path, heading to the facility's dining room.

"Well, not too much," Close to Zero suddenly noticed how clean the air was here. It's nice to get paid for your vacation in the countryside. "People from the provinces, the modernizational majority, need to be brought up to date, to be taught how to conduct polemics, explain what the country needs, something like that."

"All correct." His companion seemed satisfied with his answer. "But there is an important nuance, and I want to ask you—do you mind if I speak informally?—I want to ask you to make sure that everything that you see and hear here will never go outside of this fence. We're not asking you to sign anything, we're adults here, but you understand me, yes?"

Close to Zero nodded. They entered a dining room—it really was a dining room—but one of gargantuan dimensions—after passing through it, they ended up in a room with a television and a big vase with what looked like real sunflowers. They sat in two chairs next to a table, a woman brought them tea and an ashtray—yes, you can smoke here—and the director, looking Close to Zero in the eyes, started to talk: everything is as it should be, the mobilizational majority is gathering here; among other things, it needs lectures about current politics and about the art of polemics—oral and on the Internet, and Close to Zero is an experienced online polemicist, the types of which are hard to find. But there is one important nuance: these people, well, they're not quite… ordinary. To call them people with mental handicaps would probably be quite right, they are basically normal, but it just so happens that their cultural baggage differs (he said, "by several orders of magnitude") from the cultural baggage of the average Russian—this was probably too much of a streamlined definition, but the director decided not to frighten his guest by telling him that the group now at the facility had just last Friday finished their study of the grade-school primer with Samuil Marshak's poem, "Now you've learned your ABVs, all thirty-something of 'em."

"But why am I going on?" The director grabbed Close to Zero on the knee. "Here they are coming to dinner already; you'll see everything now for yourself."

XXIX

THE GROUP FILED into the dining room, maybe a hundred or so people, both men and women. Their ages, as it seemed to Close to Zero, varied from thirty to fifty. They were also dressed differently, but normally, we all pretty much dress like this, and Close to Zero, distracted by observing the faces and outfits, hadn't immediately noticed that the people who walked into the dining room in pair formation holding hands—man and woman, man and woman—this was strange in and of itself, but the look on their faces was so peaceful and serene, it was obvious that they felt no embarrassment that they were going to dinner as if they were in kindergarten and they themselves were little kids.

This odd crowd took their places at the table, a bell sounded, and three fat women in white smocks started to run around the room, placing big aluminum crockpots onto the tables, with "Course No. 1" written on them in red paint. Close to Zero noticed that one man or woman with a red armband sat at every table, obviously in some official role, and everyone sitting at the table would hold out their plates to them, and they poured the soup for everyone using a big ladle, and the process of pouring the soup looked very strange too—whether they were seriously worrying that they wouldn't get theirs, or just having a little fun, the people were laughing and shouting, poking at each other with their elbows, pulling each other's hair (more often men did that to women), someone was crying—and Close to Zero thought that they must be mental patients.

"So you see—ordinary people from the country," the director laid his hand on his shoulder. "At first I couldn't get used to them either, but then I got over it, even made friends with them. They're very nice, really. You know that yourself—the modernizational majority. And if they are like children—then it's your job to make sure that they grow up more quickly."

Close to Zero was silent; the director was silent too, looking into the face of the future lecturer, as if doubting whether he would get through this, then he took Close to

Zero by the hand, as if to say, "Okay, take the day off, we'll work tomorrow." A woman came up to him, took him to Building 14, a little two-story structure where on the second floor a two-room apartment had been prepared for Close to Zero. He took a shower—the towel had some words on it: "Dreams Come True," along with a logo of a state-owned corporation—then got under the blanket and fell asleep. His dreams, of course, were nightmares.

And the director couldn't get to sleep that night. He poured himself some whiskey and walked out of his room—in Building 12, across from 14—sat on a bench, and had a drink. The most detestable thing was that there was no particular need for this modernizational majority right now, and not only now; they'd done just fine without them in '07. They found enough of them to fill Luzhniki Stadium, and if needed, there were enough to fill all of Tverskaya from Manezh Square to the Belorusskaya Train Station. He had this feeling that there—the director even gestured to himself, over there—they had simply decided to play with this idiotic invention, they were so fucking interested in seeing what would happen if they injected that shit into children. It would have been better to give them to some childless foreigners, really—but now, this was sure to end badly. The director raged, went to get more whiskey, then looked at the sky, pulled out his phone and called the woman in charge of the female dormitory.

XXX

CLOSE TO ZERO had not asked anyone about anything, but long ago he figured out that he was dealing with people whose development had for some reason remained at a grade-school level—meaning it had halted, but not stopped completely. Every meeting with the kids (and he called them that—kids) left a weird impression on him; he liked talking to them, telling them about the president, the prime minister, Russia, and, for crying out loud, modernization—to see how they listened attentively to him with mouths agape, trying to remember everything he said. The phenomenal memory of his students was something he himself could envy, but they were obviously jealous of him—so intelligent and all grown-up—and even though he understood that there was something unsavory about it, he grew to like himself too. In the evenings, drinking alone in his room, he would think that that if such kidults—and there were no such creatures on the planet who fit this definition better—had appeared from somewhere, then it would make more sense to turn them into, well, I don't know, some sort of universal soldiers or suicidal terrorists. An army of fearless suicides, ready to take over the world—that would be great, but this way—well, why *them*, who needs them? Close to Zero smiled; yesterday he had given Katya and Masha an assignment—these girls could draw pretty well for their age—to design a poster for the dining room: a flag with the slogan, "Forward, Russia!" They drew it, and the poster was like a grown-up had done it, but the slogan came out as, "Fardwor, Russia!" He brought the poster to the director, who laughed, then asked him to leave the poster with him; he would show it off in Moscow and entertain a certain someone with it.

The director was the only person Close to Zero communicated with in this facility. There was also, of course, the boy Kostya, who had stayed after the lecture one time for classroom duty (he had to water the flowers, wipe the blackboard, and sweep the floor in the auditorium) and suddenly asked Close to Zero, who also hadn't left yet after the bell rang, if he had a mother. Close to Zero answered that yes, he had one, and the boy said that he did too. More to himself than to the boy, Close to Zero countered: that's strange, I thought everybody here was an orphan. Kostya knew the word "orphan" and explained that in fact, kids here have no moms or dads, but he just had no dad, his dad died when Kostya was young, but he had a mom, she just drank a lot, and once, when Kostya had gone out for a walk, he got lost, and he was picked up by a police officer, and for three days Kostya stayed at the police station, and his mom never came, and then they sent him to the orphanage.

"How many years ago was that?" Close to Zero asked Kostya, who appeared to be thirty-five years old. Kostya didn't get the question, and said, "In winter," and Close to Zero forgot about that conversation. However, after that, he started to pay more attention to Kostya than the others, to ask him how things were going, to say things especially addressed to Kostya during lectures, personally addressing Kostya, but only now it hit him—damn, what if he meant this winter?

XXXI

KOSTYA'S MOM, NADYA, took offense when she was
called an alcoholic. It was true that she had drunk up the
pension she received after the death of her husband in the
Second Chechen War, sometimes going off on binges lasting
several days, but she didn't consider herself to be a social
undesirable—she kept her home in order, it looked fine
outside too—she really wasn't a bum, she had an income,
a job working every third day as a nurse in the local Tver
Region New Jerusalem Hospital that allowed her to feed
herself and Kostya, who should have started school this year,
but didn't end up going. That time she had been drinking
for eight days or so—and when the vodka went dry, and
the money ran out she called out: "Kostya, kiddo!" but
Kostya wasn't there. She went out into the courtyard—no,

no one had seen him. The neighbors' kids were playing in the yard, she asked them if they had seen him, but no, they hadn't. She went to the police.

How was she to know that Kostya, when he went out to walk, had walked out along the train tracks and walked and walked and walked until he was exhausted? He sat down at a bus stop, fell asleep, and woke up in a room with a big window, and a police officer—a nice guy, by all appearances, was telling somebody everything about him, Kostya—said that the boy would have frozen to death if the police officer had not been coming back to work that day at exactly that time from his dacha. Kostya started to cry, the police officer and some lady there in plain clothes (it turned out that she was also a police officer) started to ask Kostya where his mom was, and he answered honestly that she was on a drinking binge, and they laughed and gave Kostya a sandwich, he ate it and fell asleep again. If he had been told that he was in Moscow, he would have been amazed, but it really was Moscow: the Levoberezhny district branch of the Department of Internal Affairs, to be precise.

It was a holiday—February 23—with a three-day weekend, and the inspector for juvenile affairs came back to work only on the Monday after they had already come from

Yaroslavl to pick up Kostya—I promised that this story would have many unfortunate coincidences, and here's another for you: in Yaroslavl, a boy from the orphanage also named Kostya went missing (actually, he drowned, but that doesn't matter, the point was that he couldn't be found), and the headmistress of the orphanage, when the police called her, decided that this Kostya who had been found in Moscow must be hers. She sent the steward of the orphanage for Kostya, and he brought him back, but it turned out it wasn't the same boy; they couldn't take him back, though, and so she kept him.

Big systems always have logistical problems.

XXXII

NADYA REALLY COULDN'T be called an alcoholic. At first she really did drink too much when her husband died, but when her son went missing she quit drinking. By the way, she believed in God but didn't prostrate herself in church; but she believed, really and truly, and she had read the Bible, though not the whole thing. And she had her own prayer, fourteen words long, in plain Russian language, not the Slavonic, and she believed that God listened in particular to these words, which meant far more to her than an "Our Father who art in Heaven" meant to some pious old church lady.

She prayed, she went to the police, she sent a photograph of Kostya to the program *Wait for Me* on Channel One (but Inna, the editor, who had worked for several talk shows, when choosing between photographs of a lost girl and Kostya, chose the girl because Inna herself had a daughter), she wrote as her status on Odnoklassniki in big letters, "MY SON IS MISSING," and they say that a friend of a friend wrote about Kostya on LiveJournal (Nadya herself didn't have a very good idea of what exactly LiveJournal was), and the post with its photograph even landed on the top of the Yandex charts of the most popular sites of the day, but still there was no response. And it was for the best that Nadya didn't read the comments under that top post, because some commenters had gone so far as to write things like—no problem, kids do go missing, you just need to birth some new ones faster, but anyway, being child-free rules.

In any case, Kostya was missing, as if he had never existed. And then something quite incomprehensible occurred in Nadya's life. Svetlana Sergeevna, a doctor of pediatric cardiology, returned from a business trip; she had gone off somewhere a month ago, and this was also strange, because what kind of business could there be that could take her away from her hospital—all of her patients are right here, and there aren't enough doctors as is. She returned from the trip and on her first day back gave Nadya a shock. She asked to bring her a photo of her deceased husband. For what, she didn't say.

Nadya herself called Edik "deceased," but until the end she did not believe that he had really been killed; they had never found his body, he had detonated a tripwire and that was it, not a trace of him remained, not even his dental crowns. Why a photograph, Svetlana Sergeevna did not explain, but Nadya wondered if he had lived. Sure enough, when she dumped out in front of the doctor a whole folder full of color photographs of her husband: matted and glossy paper, 9×12 cm and 10×15 cm—Nadya had loved back then to run off to the photo shop with the film, but then she abandoned her camera, and she had far fewer photos of Kostya than photos of her husband—Svetlana Sergeevna looked at the photos for a long time, then took off her glasses, and, looking Nadya in the eye, gravely said:

"Your husband is alive, Nadezhda. That is that."

SVETLANA SERGEEVNA herself didn't even understand where she was—it was some sort of assisted living facility, Soyuz; she saw the sign and could tell that the facility differed from, for example, a mental hospital. But nobody explained to her who those people were, what's more, they asked her not to ask anybody anything or to tell anybody anything, all that she was to do was was to make diagnoses and to prescribe treatments, but nobody had any heart ailments during this month, and all that Svetlana Sergeevna did (to be precise, not her, but the nurse Olya, a Muscovite) was measure each patient's blood pressure once a week. The patients were ordinary people, only she couldn't figure out if they were developmentally delayed or if, conversely, they were excessively active. More than anything they appeared to be shell-shocked—two years ago she had treated a shell-shocked victim from the *Nevsky Express* (the train that was blown up by terrorists), and this guy behaved the same way—his answers hadn't made sense, but he was anxious and fussy, she remembered. As such, on account of these thoughts about the concussions, she doubted whether this was really him or not, or if it was simply by association; moreover, so many years had passed, and no matter how good Svetlana Sergeevna's visual memory was, she couldn't be certain whether this was the same man who had picked up the nurse Nadya from work several years ago. The funniest thing was that she didn't remember Nadya's last name, Chernichenko or something else, and what Nadya's husband's name was, she could not remember that either. The first time she didn't ask him much at all, but the second time she couldn't resist and took him by the hand:

"Chernichenko?"

"Chernenko," Kostya answered. If only he had developed the ability to analyze his actions, he would have, of course, wondered why he had not given his name in the police station, but he was not yet able to analyze anything.

"Chernenko," he repeated, looking into the doctor's eyes. "Kostya."

That Nadya had lost her son, and that her son's name was Kostya, Svetlana Sergeevna was, of course, aware, but you can hardly blame her for not being aware of the invention of a certain Karpov, nor could she have known about the events that followed from this invention, and that the boy sitting before her was that very same seven-year old Kostya who had grown into a thirty-five-year-old man over a mere two weeks. She was sure that the man sitting before her was Kostya's dad, Nadya's husband, who said "Kostya" because he remembered his son, and she would have probably called Nadya that very day, but they had taken her cell phone from her upon her arrival at work and warned her that for the entire month she had agreed to spend there, she was not to have any contact with the outside world.

XXXIV

THERE REALLY WEREN'T enough nurses at Soyuz, and
when the recommendation from the New Jerusalem
Department of Public Health concerning "Chernenko—
Nadezhda Vitalievna—b. 1978," the director didn't even
finish reading it; he gave it to his secretary, who passed it
along and by the following day, when the Moscow-bound
bus stopped at the designated kilometer marker, Nadya
stepped up to the security gate with two regularly-sized
bags—various socks and underwear, work shoes, a book by
Darya Dontsovaya, shampoo, and other stuff like that—a
minute later her passport had been scanned by the security
guard with the battered knuckles, and ten minutes after that
Nadya's career at Soyuz ended as quickly as it had begun. It
wasn't her fault, Svetlana Sergeevna had explained to her

in great detail everything that she knew about the strictness of the regime there; but who could have known that at that very moment the children would be walking along to breakfast in pairs and that one of the children, actually not a child, of course, but a grown man, would suddenly push off of the woman next to him, break away from the formation, and run up to Nadya, crying out, "Mom!"

Of course it seemed to her that she had lost her mind. Up to her was running, well, yeah, Edik, Svetlana Sergeevna was not mistaken, but Edik for some reason was shouting out "Mom" but not "Nadya."

"Mom!" he shouted, and Nadya did not notice the fact that for an ordinary, though specialized, assisted living facility, there sure were a lot of security guards—young men in identical black suits and ties sprang out from every corner of the premises and ran toward her and to the one who was shouting at her. Two of the men apprehended the man, two got Nadya, and she saw no one else but these two security guards. They led her to the security gate, sat her next to their colleague who had scanned her passport, and told her to wait.

Nadya cried. She did not understand and could not understand what had happened, but the director immediately understood when the on-duty officer in charge of security appeared in his office without knocking and reported: some woman had arrived with a nurse's ID, but then it turned out, judging from all appearances, that she was the mother of one of the students. The director cursed—he had suspected from the very beginning that something like this could happen, but had not come to any conclusions about what to do about it. He asked where the woman was being held and stepped into the waiting room. After a second he returned, poured himself a whiskey, then pulled a piece of gum out of his pocket, stuck it in his mouth, and again walked out of the office.

XXXV

NADYA, OF COURSE, didn't believe it when the man in the jacket, but without a tie, told her that she had just imagined it all, and that there was no husband here, and that one of the deranged patients ("They really didn't warn you? The rehabilitation of the mentally ill is taking place here.") had thrown himself at her thinking that she was his mother, whom he had himself killed with an ax the year before—that's the point of why they are crazy, they do things like throw themselves at people. But the director didn't ask her to believe him, he simply told her that she would receive pay for a month's work, but, given what had happened, she would not be working here, and as long as she didn't tell anyone about what she had seen and heard here, everything would be fine. "But if you do…" the director added, but she did not understand this "But if," she just understood that in spite of his smile, he was threatening her.

"Let me see him," she asked, but the director again smiled and repeated that he was sorry, that she hadn't understood him, and that he was counting on her common sense or else "there would be a problem." He also offered up a car to take her home, as the next bus wouldn't come until the evening. Nadya dried her eyes and nodded. She thought to herself, "Look what I've drunk myself into."

Close to Zero immediately noticed that Kostya wasn't at the lecture, and when he asked about him, the children began interrupting as if trying to outshout one another that Kostya's mom had come. "He's with his mom?" Close to Zero inquired, but the children didn't know the specifics, and only the gossiper Katya (the one who had co-authored with quiet Misha the famed "Fardwor, Russia!") said that no, Kostya wasn't with his mom, they had taken her off somewhere, and that they had beaten Kostya, and now he was in the medical ward. Close to Zero almost started to cry, he wanted to do something, and he told the children that today he wanted them to play "Cities" among them-selves, but then he remembered that these children didn't know any cities, and he then pulled himself back together and had them play a word game. He explained the rules and then left.

The director was not in his office. Close to Zero ran into him on the stairway of the administrative building. He dragged Close to Zero back into his office, closed the door behind them, poured a whiskey for himself and for his guest, and (in the tabloids they describe such moments with the expression, "unable to hold back his tears") described the situation. By all indications, they were in an emergency situation.

XXXVI

THE CO-OWNER OF FALANSTER, Boris Kupriyanov, was manning the cash register when Close to Zero walked up to pay for *Mutants* by Armand Marie Leroi. Kupriyanov asked him where he'd been, but the buyer only waved his hand: oh, don't ask. When they killed Kostya, Close to Zero came to the director and said that he wanted to go home and was even prepared to refuse compensation for his lectures, especially since he had not managed to get to the lecture on Internet polemics. The director said that he understood and that he was counting on his common sense, and the money, of course, would be paid all the same; and he recommended he take the money and go on vacation somewhere like Turkey. "Most importantly, don't drink," he added for some reason. Close to Zero said nothing in reply; but on that day, or to be precise, from that day on, he felt like a nightmarish ghoul. He didn't go to Turkey, and he also, of course, contradicted the director's *most important* recommendation, albeit in absentia: he drank and drank and drank, and when he was tired of drinking, he remembered that books existed, and he headed to Gnezdnikovsky. He saw the cover of *Mutants* and almost laughed out loud—the jury is still out on who's really a mutant.

He walked along Tverksaya looking at the ground as he went, took the underground crosswalk to Manezh Square, made his way to the statue of Marshall Zhukov, and called the commander a butcher, then walked onto Red Square and for some reason headed into GUM.

Some kind of scandalous scene was taking place in GUM. A young salesgirl was crying, she was very beautiful and well put-together. Close to Zero knew this type—they sell expensive junk and then at some point start to believe that this luxury is part of their own cheap little lives. They begin to look down on their shoppers as if they were shit, and if some kind of shittily dressed woman starts to cry it only means that justice has been served. Close to Zero looked all around. Justice had taken the form of a doe-eyed, curly-haired brunette, maybe in her forties, who was shouting something apparently important. Close to Zero listened more closely but heard nothing except "a vest from Yarmak" and "I am a reporter of international standing." But to him this was enough, this one word: "reporter." Puzzle solved.

XXXVII

HER NAME WAS BECKY, that is to say that it was probably something different, but if a girl asks to be called by some other name, when it's all said and done, why not. She worked for a popular newspaper and had achieved some success, but she hadn't had a front-page story that would mark her name in the annals of international journalism, and though she didn't admit it to herself out loud, she suffered because of this and felt underappreciated. The only thing that she asked Close to Zero was why he himself didn't write about this, he's also a writer, but he only laughed—there are easier ways to commit suicide, so why go looking for it. He nevertheless agreed to talk into the recorder, and he told everything: what he had seen, what the director had told him that awful day (that is, about the serum; he, however, didn't mention

Karpov's name—it wasn't certain that the director himself knew it), and about the director himself, who in his normal life worked in a "Center for Social-Conservative Politics."

Becky wrote it all down, and sighed when he got to the part about Nadya, she even cried a little bit, then made a note to herself in the recorder, "New Jerusalem, hospital," and then was rude to the waiter for some reason and ran off in a huff. Close to Zero drank the rest of his coffee and headed home to read *Mutants*.

Becky quickly found Nadya, but Nadya, who had sworn to herself that she would not tell anyone what had happened to her at the assisted living facility (after this incident, she and Svetlana Sergeevna had not talked at all, and the doctor understood that they had probably scared her and made her sign an agreement), for some reason immediately believed this woman and told her everything—thank heavens, Becky didn't tell her about the serum or what Kostya had turned into, nor that Kostya was now dead. She recorded Nadya's story, gave her a Globus Gourmet chocolate bar that she had bought earlier, and headed home. Passing by the gate to Soyuz, she stopped and photographed the sign with her iPhone, and then continued on her way. No more loose ends remain; you can have a seat for the final report.

XXXVIII

"YOU KNOW WHY I gave you the interview? Because you've never sucked up to anybody for anything," Becky read on a banner hanging over the door to the editor-in-chief's office. To one side of the banner were six photographs framed in black as if in mourning with the caption, "We are proud of you, and we remember you." It all looked creepy, but first and foremost, this newspaper was read and cited throughout the world, and then secondly, their very own editor (at one point he had worked at *Kommersant* as the head of the accidents and emergencies desk and his catchphrase, "We fucked your Biennale," which had been addressed to a colleague from the Cultural Bureau, still characterized him better than any other words), having read Becky's text, told her that jokes about drugs were a bad idea, but even if this wasn't drugs, it was still something he wouldn't print, because it may be all the same to her, but he didn't want to have to swallow dust in courtrooms for the rest of his life. She shrugged—what a fool—and gave us a call here.

This editor, on the contrary, liked it all, he only suggested adding a conclusion to the end: "The scum of Putin's stagnation closed in over their heads," and Becky didn't object—well, let it be scum, then. When Becky left, the editor changed the headline from "A Children's Farm Under the Banner of Modernization" to the scathing, "Fardwor, Russia!"—he had been told about the contentious nature of this journalist, and he was afraid to give her another reason to yell at him, he really didn't like to be yelled at.

The newspaper came out on Monday and, though they screamed about it on the Echo of Moscow radio station— they know how to turn any minutia from the newspapers into an event of global proportions—the sky didn't fall to the earth, nor did any high-profile resignations occur, *nothing* really changed, in fact, and Becky, stirring her tea with a spoon, thought about what would have happened if, say, she had been able to prove, for example, that the FSB had blown up that building in Moscow in '99. She looked at the brown surface of the tea as it settled down after being stirred and understood that no, no, nothing would have happened, nothing at all.

But toward Wednesday some underground wheels finally went into motion. The article was reprinted by the London *Times*, and the same morning the news about the children's farm made the CNN headlines; that evening the press service of the Russian president reported on a telephone conversation between Dmitry Medvedev and Barack Obama: "The development of bilateral relations and a scientific-technological partnership were discussed."

And on Thursday morning in the offices of the state corporation that owned Soyuz a press conference took place with Health Minister Onishchenko, and Onishchenko (not mentioning Becky's article) confessed—yes, yes, confessed!—that, in fact, the assisted living facility, closed for quarantine, was being used for the rehabilitation of children stricken by the flu. "Children, ladies and gentlemen," repeated the health minister, "I want you to draw your attention to this—children, and children are like grownups, but small. Boys, in contrast to grown-up men, don't sport beards, and girls, in contrast to grown-up women, don't have breasts. Have I explained this clearly?" The press secretary of the corporation, smiling, told the journalists that a bus was waiting for them outside, and anyone who felt so inclined could go to Novaya Riga after the press conference and see with their own eyes what was going on at the facility. To get from the corporation's office in the southwest of Moscow to Soyuz, which was on the far northwestern side of town, was a long ride, but they had blocked Leninsky and Leningradsky Prospects for the journalists' bus, which was escorted by cars from the DPS, and Becky, looking out from her apartment's window onto the emptied Tverskaya, wrote on her Twitter: "Make way, peasants, the louse is on the march." She thought that it was someone from the Russian top brass.

XXXIX

THE JOURNALISTS WERE showed around the assisted
living facility by the director himself. Yes, until that summer
he really had worked in the Social-Conservative Center,
but now he had decided to walk away from politics, and
he was trying a new role for himself, and plus they pay
better at the state corporation. "The terrible thing about
the tabloids is that they mix the facts and lies, and it's hard
to separate the two," he sighed, showing the journalists
the living quarters, where children were sniffling in their
small beds, real little children who didn't look anything like
forty-year-old men or thirty-year-old women. "Is there a
Kostya Chernenko among them, seven years old?" someone
asked. "No, no such kid," the director sighed again. "When
I read that, I checked our database to see if we had a boy

by that name. No, and that's the truth. Pass that along to that Becky!"

There were enough people seeking to pass something along to Becky, however, even without this. That same morning her editor called—the one who had the quote about the Biennale—and told her that they would obviously be opening a criminal case up against her, and if she could, then she should get away before she received the summons. She had been expecting something like this, she had even dreamt about it, and she wasn't scared at all, although she had thought that it was better to take care of her backup plans before the publication than after.

However, there was someone who could stand up for her. Or not really to "stand up," but at least to help her with advice—yes, there was one person. But the voice on the phone giggled, "The number you have dialed is temporarily unavailable, please try again," and Becky suddenly felt terrified, and although ten minutes later she finally got through to Kirill, I want this episode with her dialed number not answering to remain so that you could understand what Becky was going through that morning.

When she and Kirill met at The Bridge restaurant at a party celebrating the hundredth anniversary of a certain newspaper, he told her right away that if she planned to marry an oligarch, then she should find someone else—he wasn't going to marry, he already had children in America and Dagestan, and he hadn't yet come up with how he was going to advise them to take care of his money in their inheritances. "My brother recently died, you probably heard about that," he said, bending toward her, "Now I have to carry the weight of all that on my shoulders, and it is quite difficult." She dabbed her eyes with a napkin—yes, she had heard about Mefody Magomedov's sudden unexpected death, she had even wanted to write a report from the funeral, but she hadn't been able to find out where and how he was buried; only later, a special press release from the Vremya-Kapital Corporation reported that Mefody had been buried in the family tomb in Derbent's Russian cemetery. They were silent for a moment. Then she went to his place. After that they met—well, how many times, probably eight— but those dates were enough for her to feel happy. She was, seemingly, really in love.

Kirill listened to her silently and then laughed—yeah, you've gone and done it now—but she could see that he was proud of her. He called an assistant and said to move all of his meetings until five in the afternoon, and then drove her to Vnukovo-3 himself. Make way, peasants!

Within an hour that same Falcon 7X was carrying her off somewhere in the direction of the United Kingdom of Great Britain and Northern Ireland, and after another several hours, she wrote on her Twitter that she was "laying around at a hacienda outside of London." The next morning a printout of this tweet was lying on the table of the director of the FSB.

XL

"KARPOV, HEAD TO THE EXIT with your things," reported, grimacing, the same FSB agent who had rung at his door two months ago after Elena Nikolaevna had left. Karpov was standing in the corridor naked to the waist, looking not at his guest but at a mirror—while detained in this apartment, not shaving, he had grown a funny-looking beard. "Where are we going?" he asked while dressing. "Where do you wanna go?" the *chekist* answered lightheartedly, and Karpov for some reason immediately believed that he was being released.

"Do you have money for a taxi?" his companion asked when Karpov, squinting in the daylight, looked around as trying to figure out where they were waiting for him.

"I'll take a *marshrutka*," he snapped and marched down Dzerzhinsky Street. The chekist silently watched him walk off.

When he put the key in the door, it turned out that the apartment was locked from the inside. He was hesitant to ring the bell—the events of the last month had made him kind of nervous. But the door opened on its own, and there, smiling and crying, stood Marina.

"Karpov," Marina said, "We're having a boy, though it apparently isn't yours."

"You'll have mine someday," Karpov stepped across the threshold and hugged his wife. The prospect of raising an heir to the oligarch bloodline of Magomedovs seemed even funny to him, and all in all, he was terribly glad to see his wife. He loved her, by the way.

XLI

THEY FLEW TO MOSCOW early the next morning; Marina slept, and Karpov looked back and forth, first at her, then at the clouds, and smiled. During those days spent locked up, he discovered that he could see into the future, and he knew everything now:

Becky would stay in London; she would marry some Hindu and stop dreaming about headlines.

The project for the accelerated growth of the modernizational majority would be recognized as a mistake and would lead to some high-profile resignations in the presidential administration and in the United Russia political party.

As a result of those resignations, at least two bright and shining new leaders would appear among the ranks of the nonsystemic opposition who, however, would also fail to increase the political influence of oppositional organizations in any fundamental manner.

The Federal Target Program "A Well-Fed Russia" would ultimately become a huge corporate scandal, as a result of which just one person would end up behind bars, the corresponding member of the Russian Academy of Natural Sciences, Elena Nikolaevna Gorskaya, who, however, would be amnestied quickly thereafter in celebration of the seventieth anniversary of the Great Victory.

The big children to whom Close to Zero had given his lectures would never be seen again, and the assisted living facility Soyuz would again open its welcoming doors to the laborers of the oil and gas industry for whom, in fact, it had been built.

Nadya Chernenko, even before that, within a week, would end up in a mental asylum and really would lose her mind, but in that order—first, she'd get there, then she'd lose it.

Kirill Magomedov would unexpectedly agree to head up the Olympstroi Corporation, even though he knew it to be an unfavorable proposition for him, and would lead it for a record amount of time—up until the 2014 Olympics.

The Olympics would take place in Korea—the International Olympic Committee would review its own decision due to the worsening situation in the region of the Russian–Georgian conflict.

During the time that the situation would be worsening again in the region of the Russian-Georgian conflict, the newspapers would write about a strange occurrence in the Georgian city of Gori—how soldiers who had gone astray from the Russian contingent attacked a toy store, brutally murdering a salesgirl and a security guard, and, returning fire, retreated to the separation line, but then it would turn out that nothing had been stolen from the store but a stuffed Kopatych doll.

A modernizational majority would form all by itself and would vote in the 2012 elections for that national leader of the two whom the leaders themselves would pick in a simple game of drawing matchsticks.

And that no one would ever remember any of this.

When the plane touched the ground, the passengers applauded and Marina woke up. At this airport, instead of ramps they used telescopic tubes with ads for Sberbank with a new logo—Marina saw it for the first time and, stopping, tried to think of how it was different than the old one.

"Hey, what's with you, go on." Karpov lightly pushed her in the back. "Go on," he repeated. "We've arrived."

Marina turned and kissed her husband, and the scum of stagnation closed in over their heads.